Rinehart   The After House

The After House

Also available by Mary Roberts
Rinehart:

The Album
The Case of Jennie Brice
The Circular Staircase
Episode of the Wandering Knife
The State vs. Elinor Norton
The Swimming Pool
The Wall

The After House

Mary Roberts Rinehart

G.K.HALL&CO.

Boston, Massachusetts

1981

Library of Congress Cataloging in Publication Data

Rinehart, Mary Roberts, 1876-1958.
   The after house.

   Large print ed.
   1. Large type books.   I. Title.
   [PS3535.I73A7   1981]   813'.52   81-306
   ISBN 0-8161-3236-4   AACR1

Published in Large Print by arrangement with
Holt, Rinehart & Winston, Inc.

Set in Penta / Mergenthaler Linotron 202
18 pt Times Roman by Modern Graphics, Inc.

Contents

RINE

"A hodge-podge of characters, motives, passions, all working together toward that terrible night of August twelfth, nineteen hundred and eleven, when hell seemed loose on a painted sea."

Chapter 1

I Plan a Voyage

By the bequest of an elder brother, I was left enough money to see me through a small college in Ohio, and to secure me four years in a medical school in the East. Why I chose medicine I hardly know. Possibly the career of a surgeon attracted the adventurous element in me. Perhaps, coming of a family of doctors, I merely followed the line of least resistance. It may be, indirectly but inevitably, that I might be on the yacht *Ella* on that terrible night of August 12, more than a year ago.

I got through somehow. I played quarterback on the football team, and made some money coaching. In summer I did whatever came to hand from chartering a sail-boat at a summer resort and taking passengers, at so much a

1

head, to checking up cucumbers in Indiana for a Western pickle house.

I was practically alone. Commencement left me with a diploma, a new dress-suit, an out-of-date medical library, a box of surgical instruments of the same date as the books, and an incipient case of typhoid fever.

I was twenty-four, six feet tall, and forty inches around the chest. Also, I had lived clean, and worked and played hard. I got over the fever finally, pretty much all bone and appetite, but — alive. Thanks to the college, my hospital care had cost nothing. It was a good thing: I had just seven dollars in the world.

The yacht *Ella* lay in the river not far from my hospital windows. She was not a yacht when I first saw her, nor at any time, technically, unless I use the word in the broad sense of a pleasure-boat. She was a two-master, and, when I saw her first, as dirty and disreputable as are most coasting-vessels. Her rejuvenation was the history of my convalescence. On the day she stood forth in her coat of white paint, I exchanged my dressing-gown for clothing that, however loosely it hung, was still clothing. Her new sails marked my promotion to beefsteak, her brass rails and awnings my first independent excursion up and down the corridor outside my door, and, incidentally, my return to a collar and tie.

The river shipping appealed to me, to my imagination, clean washed by my illness and ready as a child's for new impressions: liners gliding down to the bay and the open sea; shrewish, scolding tugs; dirty but picturesque tramps. My enthusiasm amused the nurses, whose ideas of adventure consisted of little jaunts of exploration into the abdominal cavity, and whose aseptic minds revolted at the sight of dirty sails.

One day I pointed out to one of them an old schooner, red and brown, with patched canvas spread, moving swiftly down the river before a stiff breeze.

"Look at her!" I exclaimed. "There goes adventure, mystery, romance! I should like to be sailing on her."

"You would have to boil the drinking-

3

water," she replied dryly. "And the ship is probably swarming with rats."

"Rats," I affirmed, "add to the local color. Ships are their native habitat. Only sinking ships don't have them."

But her answer was to retort that rats carried bubonic plague, and to exit, carrying the sugar-bowl. I was ravenous, as are all convalescent typhoids, and one of the ways in which I eked out my still slender diet was by robbing the sugar-bowl at meals.

That day, I think it was, the deck furniture was put out on the *Ella* — numbers of white wicker chairs and tables, with bright cushions to match the awnings. I had a pair of ancient opera-glasses, as obsolete as my amputating knives, and, like them, a part of my heritage. By that time I felt a proprietary interest in the *Ella*, and through my glasses, carefully focused with a pair of scissors, watched the arrangement of the deck furnishings. A girl was directing the men. I judged, from the poise with which she carried herself, that she was attractive — and knew it. How beautiful

4

she was, and how well she knew it, I was to find out before long. McWhirter to the contrary, she had nothing to do with my decision to sign as a sailor on the *Ella*.

One of the bright spots of that long hot summer was McWhirter. We had graduated together in June, and in October he was to enter a hospital in Buffalo as a resident. But he was as indigent as I, and from June to October is four months.

"Four months," he said to me. "Even at two meals a day, boy, that's something over two hundred and forty. And I can eat four times a day, without a struggle! Wouldn't you think one of these overworked-for-the-good-of-humanity dubs would take a vaction and give me a chance to hold down his practice?"

Nothing of the sort developing, McWhirter went into a drugstore, and managed to pull through the summer with unimpaired cheerfulness, confiding to me that he secured his luncheons free at the soda counter. He came frequently to see me, bringing always a pocketful of chewing gum, which he assured me was excellent to allay the gnawings of hunger, and later, as my condition warranted it, small bags of gum-drops and other pharmacy confections.

McWhirter it was who got me my berth on the *Ella*. It must have been about the 20th of July, for the *Ella* sailed on the 28th. I was strong enough to leave the hospital, but not yet physically able for any prolonged exertion. McWhirter, who was short and stout, had been alternately flirting with the nurse, as she moved in and out preparing my room for the night, and sizing me up through narrowed eyes.

"No," he said, evidently following a private line of thought; "you don't belong behind a counter, Leslie. I'm darned if I think you belong in the medical profession, either. The British army'd suit you."

"The — what?"

"You know — Kipling idea — riding horseback, head of a column — undress uniform — colonel's wife making eyes at you — leading last hopes and all that.''

''The British army with Kipling trimmings being out of the question, the original issue is still before us. I'll have to work, Mac, and work like the devil, if I'm to feed myself.''

There being no answer to this, McWhirter contented himself with eyeing me.

''I'm thinking,'' I said, ''of going to Europe. The sea is calling me, Mac.''

''So was the grave a month ago, but it didn't get you. Don't be an ass, boy. How are you going to sea?''

''Before the mast.'' This apparently conveying no meaning to McWhirter, I supplemented — ''as a common sailor.''

He was indignant at first, offering me his room and a part of his small salary until I got my strength; then he became dubious; and finally, so well did I paint my picture of long, idle days on the ocean, of sweet, cool nights under the stars, with breezes that purred through the sails, rocking the ship to slumber — finally he waxed enthusiastic, and was even for giving up the pharmacy at once and sailing with me.

He had been fitting out the storeroom of a sailing-yacht with drugs, he informed me, and doing it under the personal direction of the owner's wife.

"I've made a hit with her," he confided. "Since she's learned I'm a graduate M.D., she's letting me do the whole thing. I've made up some lotions to prevent sunburn, and that seasick prescription of old Larimer's and she thinks I'm the whole cheese. I'll suggest you as ship's doctor."

"How many men in the crew?"

"Eight, I think, or ten. It's a small boat, and carries a small crew."

"Then they don't want a ship's doctor. If I go, I'll go as a sailor," I said firmly. "And I want your word, Mac, not a word about me, except that I am honest."

"You'll have to wash decks, probably."

"I am filled with a wild longing to wash decks," I asserted, smiling at his disturbed face. "I should probably also have to polish brass. There's a great deal of brass on the boat.''

''How do you know that?''

When I told him, he was much excited, and although it was dark and the *Ella* consisted of three lights, he insisted on the opera-glasses, and was persuaded when he saw her. Finally he put down the glasses and came over to me.

''Perhaps you are right, Leslie,'' he said soberly. ''You don't want charity, any more than they want a ship's doctor. Wherever you go and whatever you do, whether you're swabbing decks in your bare feet or polishing brass railings with an old sick, you're a man.''

He was more moved than I had ever seen him, and ate a gum-drop to cover his embarrassment. Soon after that he took his departure, and the following day he telephoned to say that, if the sea was still calling me, he could get a note to the captain recommending me. I asked him to get the note.

Good old Mac! The sea was calling me, true enough, but only dire necessity was driving me to ship before the mast — necessity and perhaps what, for want of a better name, we call destiny. For what is fate but inevitable law, inevitable consequence.

The stirring of my blood, generations removed from a seafaring ancestor; my illness, not a cause, but a result; McWhirter, filling prescriptions behind the glass screen of a pharmacy, and fitting out, in porcelain jars, the medicine-closet of the *Ella*; Turner and his wife, Schwartz, the mulatto Tom, Singleton, and Elsa Lee; all thrown together, a hodge-podge of characters, motives, passions, and hereditary tendencies, through an inevitable law working together toward that terrible night of August 12, when hell seemed loose on a painted sea.

Chapter 2

The Painted Ship

The *Ella* had been a coasting-vessel, carrying dressed lumber to South America, and on her return trip bringing a miscellaneous cargo — hides and wool, sugar from Pernambuco, whatever offered. The firm of Turner and Sons owned the line of which the *Ella* was one of the smallest vessels.

The gradual elimination of sailing-ships and the substitution of steamers in the coasting-trade, left the *Ella*, with others, out of commission. She was still seaworthy, rather fast, as such vessels go, and steady. Marshall Turner, the oldest son of old Elias Turner, the founder of the business, bought it at a nominal sum, with the intention of using it as a private yacht. And, since it was a superstition of the house never to change the name of one of its vessels, the schooner *Ella,* odorous of fresh lumber or raw rubber, as the case might be, dingy gray in color, with slovenly decks on which lines of seamen's clothing were generally hanging to dry, remained, in her metamorphosis, still the *Ella.*

Marshall Turner was a wealthy man, but he equipped his new pleasure-boat very modestly. As few changes as were possible were made. He increased the size of the forward house, adding quarters for the captain and the two mates, and thus kept the after house for himself and his friends. He fumigated the hold and the forecastle—a precaution that kept all the crew coughing for two days, and drove them out of the odor of formaldehyde to the deck to sleep. He installed an electric lighting and refrigerating plant, put a bath in the forecastle, to the bewilderment of the men, who were inclined to think it a reflection on their habits, and almost entirely rebuilt, inside, the old officers' quarters in the after house.

The wheel, replaced by a new one, white and gilt, remained in its old position behind the after house, the steersman standing on a raised iron grating above the wash of the deck. Thus from the chart-room, which had become a sort of lounge and card-room, through a small barred window it was possible to see the man at the wheel, who, in his turn, commanded a view of part of the chart-room, but not of the floor.

The craft was schooner-rigged, carried three lifeboats and a collapsible raft, and was navigated by a captain, first and second mates, and a crew of six able-bodied sailors and one gaunt youth whose sole knowledge of navigation had been gained on an Atlantic City catboat. Her destination was vague — Panama perhaps, possibly a South American port, depending on the weather and the whim of the owner.

I do not recall that I performed the nautical rite of signing articles. Armed with the note McWhirter had secured for me, and with what I fondly hoped was the rolling gait of the seafaring man, I approached the captain — a bearded and florid individual. I had dressed the part — old trousers, a cap, and a sweater from which I had removed my college letter. McWhirter, who had supervised my preparations, and who had accompanied me to the wharf, suggested that I omit my morning shave. The result was, as I look back, a lean and cadaverous six-foot youth, with the hospital pallor still on him, his chin covered with a day's beard, his hair cropped short, and a cannibalistic gleam in his eyes. I remember that my wrists, thin and bony, annoyed me, and that the girl I had seen through the opera-glasses came on board, and stood off, detached and indifferent, but with her eyes on me, while the captain read my letter.

When he finished, he held it out to me.

"I've got my crew," he said curtly.

"There isn't — I suppose there's no chance of your needing another hand?"

"No." He turned away, then glanced back at the letter I was still holding,

14

rather dazed. "You can leave your name and address with the mate over there. If anything turns up he'll let you know."

My address! The hospital?

I folded the useless letter and thrust it into my pocket. The captain had gone forward, and the girl with the cool eyes was leaning against the rail, watching me.

"You are the man Mr. McWhirter has been looking after, aren't you?"

"Yes." I pulled off my cap, and, recollecting myself — "Yes, miss."

"You are not a sailor?"

"I have had some experience — and I am willing."

"You have been ill, haven't you?"

"Yes — miss."

"Could you polish brass, and things like that?"

"I could try. My arms are strong enough. It is only when I walk —"

But she did not let me finish. She left the rail abruptly, and disappeared down the companionway into the after house. I waited uncertainly. The captain saw me still loitering, and scowled. A procession

15

of men with trunks jostled me; a colored man, evidently a butler, ordered me out of his way while he carried down into the cabin, with almost reverent care, a basket of wine.

When the girl returned, she came to me, and stood for a moment, looking me over with cool, appraising eyes. I had been right about her appearance: she was charming — or no, hardly charming. She was too aloof for that. But she was beautiful, an Irish type, with blue-gray eyes and almost black hair. The tilt of her head was haughty. Later I came to know that her *hauteur* was indifference: but at first I was frankly afraid of her, afraid of her cool, mocking eyes and the upward thrust of her chin

"My brother-in-law is not here," she said after a moment, "but my sister is below in the cabin. She will speak to the captain about you. Where are your things?"

I glanced toward the hospital, where my few wordly possessions, including my dress clothes, my amputating set, and such of my books as I had not been able to sell, were awaiting dispositon. "Very near, miss," I said.

"Better bring them at once; we are sailing in the morning." She turned away as if to avoid my thanks, but stopped and came back.

"We are taking you as a sort of extra man," she explained. "You will work with the crew, but it is possible that we will need you — do you know anything about butler's work?"

I hesitated. If I said yes, and then failed —

"I could try."

"I thought, from your appearance, perhaps you had done something of the sort." Oh, shades of my medical forebears, who had bequeathed me, along with the library, what I had hoped was a professional manner! "The butler is a poor sailor. If he fails us, you will take his place."

She gave a curt little nod of dismissal, and I went down the gangplank and along the wharf. I had secured what I went for; my summer was provided for, and I was still seven dollars to the good.

I was exultant, but with my exultation was mixed a curious anger at McWhirter, that he had advised me not to shave that morning.

My preparation took little time. Such of my wardrobe as was worth saving, McWhirter took charge of. I sold the remainder of my books, and in a sailor's outfitting-shop I purchased boots and slickers — the sailors' oilskins. With my last money I bought a good revolver, second-hand, and cartridges. I was glad later that I had bought the revolver, and that I had taken with me the surgical instruments, antiquated as they were, which, in their mahogany case, had accompanied my grandfather through the Civil War, and had done, as he was wont to chuckle, as much damage as a three-pounder. McWhirter came to the wharf with me, and looked the *Ella* over with eyes of proprietorship.

"Pretty snappy-looking boat," he said. "If the butler gets sick, give him some of my seasick remedy. And take care of yourself, boy." He shook hands, his open face flushed with emotion.

"Darned shame to see you going like this. Don't eat too much, and don't fall in love with any of the women. Good-by."

He started away, and I turned toward the ship; but a moment later I heard him calling me. He came back, rather breathless.

"Up in my neighborhood, he panted, "they say Turner is a devil. Whatever happens, it's not your mix-in. Better — better tuck your gun under your mattress and forget you've got it. You've got some disposition yourself."

The *Ella* sailed the following day at ten o'clock. She carried nineteen people, of whom five were the Turners and their guests. The cabin was full of flowers and steamer-baskets.

Thirty-one days later she came into port again, a lifeboat covered with canvas trailing at her stern.

Chapter 3

I Unclench My Hands

From the first the captain disclaimed responsibility for me. I was housed in the forecastle, and ate with the men. There, however, my connection with the crew and the navigation of the ship ended. Perhaps it was as well, although I resented it at first. I was weaker than I had thought, and dizzy at the mere thought of going aloft.

As a matter of fact, I found myself a sort of decksteward, given the responsibility of looking after the shuffle-board and other deck games, the steamer-rugs, the cards — for they played bridge steadily — and answerable to George Williams, the butler, for the various liquors served on deck.

The work was easy, and the situation rather amused me. After an effort or two to bully me, one of which resulted in my holding him over the rail until he turned gray with fright, Williams treated me as an equal, which was gratifying.

The weather was good, the food fair. I had no reason to repent my bargain. Of the sailing qualities of the *Ella* there could be no question. The crew, selected by Captain Richardson from the best men of the Turner line, knew their business, and, especially after the Williams incident, made me one of themselves. Barring the odor of formaldehyde in the forecastle, which drove me to sleeping on deck for a night or two, everything was going smoothly, at least on the surface.

Smoothly as far as the crew was concerned. I was not so sure about the after house.

As I have said, owing to the small size of the vessel, and the fact that considerable of the space had been used for baths, there were, besides the family, only two guests, a Mrs. Johns, a *divorcée,* and a Mr. Vail. Mrs. Turner and Miss Lee shared the services of a maid, Karen Hansen, who, with a stewardess, Henrietta Sloane, occupied a double cabin. Vail had a small room, as had Turner, with a bath between which they used in common. Mrs. Turner's room was a large one, with its own bath, into which Elsa Lee's room also opened. Mrs. Johns had a room and bath. Roughly, and not drawn to scale, the living quarters of the family were arranged like the diagram on page 217.

I have said that things were not going smoothly in the after house. I felt it rather than saw it. The women rose late — except Miss Lee, who was frequently about when I washed the deck. They chatted and laughed together, read, played bridge when the men were so inclined, and now and then, when their attention was drawn to it, looked at the sea. They were always exquisitely and carefully dressed, and I looked at them as I would at any other masterpieces of creative art, with nothing of covetousness in my admiration.

The men were violently opposed types — Turner, tall, heavy-shouldered, morose by habit, with a prominent nose and rapidly thinning hair, and with strong, pale-blue eyes, congested from hard drinking; Vail, shorter by three inches, dark, good-looking, with that dusky flush under the skin which shows good red blood, and as temperate as Turner was dissipated.

Vail was strong, too. After I had held Williams over the rail I turned to find him looking on, amused. And when the frightened butler had taken himself, muttering threats, to the galley, Vail came over to me and ran his hand down my arm.

"Where did you get it?" he asked.

"Oh, I've always had some muscle," I said. "I'm in bad shape now; just getting over fever."

"Fever, eh? I thought it was jail. Look here."

He threw out his biceps for me to feel. It was a ball of iron under my fingers. The man was as strong as an ox. He smiled at my surprise, and, after looking to see that no one was in sight, offered to mix me a highball from a decanter and siphon on a table.

I refused.

It was his turn to be surprised.

"I gave it up when I was in train —
in the hospital," I corrected myself. "I
find I don't miss it."

He eyed me with some curiosity over
his glass, and, sauntering away, left me
to my work of folding rugs. But when I
had finished, and was chalking the deck
for shuffle-board, he joined me again,
dropping his voice, for the women had
come up by that time and were
breakfasting on the lee side of the after
house.

"Have you any idea, Leslie, how
much whisky there is on board?"

"Williams has considerable, I believe.
I don't think there is any in the forward
house. The captain is a teetotaler."

"I see. When these decanters go back,
Williams takes charge of them?"

"Yes. He locks them away."

He dropped his voice still lower.

"Empty them, Leslie," he said. "Do
you understand? Throw what is left
overboard. And, if you get a chance at

William's key, pitch a dozen or two quarts overboard.''

''And be put in irons!''

''Not necessarily. I think you understand me. I don't trust Williams. In a week we could have this boat fairly dry.''

''There is a great deal of wine.''

He scowled. ''Damn Williams, anyhow! His instructions were — but never mind about that. Get rid of the whisky.''

Turner coming up the companionway at that moment, Vail left me. I had understood him perfectly. It was common talk in the forecastle that Turner was drinking hard, and that, in fact, the cruise had been arranged by his family in the hope that, away from his clubs, he would alter his habits — a fallacy, of course. Taken away from his customary daily round, given idle days on a summer sea, and aided by Williams, the butler, he was drinking his head off.

Early as it was, he was somewhat the worse for it that morning. He made directly for me. It was the first time he had noticed me, although it was the third day out. He stood in front of me, his red eyes flaming, and, although I am a tall man, he had an inch perhaps the advantage of me.

"What's this about Williams?" he demanded furiously. "What do you mean by a thing like that?"

"He was bullying me. I didn't intend to drop him."

The ship was rolling gently; he made a pass at me with a magazine he carried, and almost lost his balance. The women had risen, and were watching from the corner of the after house. I caught him and steadied him until he could clutch a chair.

"You try any tricks like that again, and you'll go overboard," he stormed. "Who are you, anyhow? Not one of our men?"

I saw the quick look between Vail and Mrs. Turner, and saw her come forward. Mrs. Johns followed her, smiling.

"Marsh!" Mrs. Turner protested. "I told you about him — the man who had been ill.''

''Oh, another of your friends!'' he sneered, and looked from me to Vail with his ugly smile.

Vail went rather pale and threw up his head quickly. The next moment Mrs. Johns had saved the situation with a irrelevant remark, and the incident was over. They were playing bridge, not without dispute, but at least without insult. But I had had a glimpse beneath the surface of that luxurious cruise, one of many such in the next few days.

That was on Monday, the third day out. Up to that time Miss Lee had not noticed me, except once, when she found me scrubbing the deck, to comment on a corner that she thought might be cleaner, and another time in the evening, when she and Vail sat in chairs until late, and she had sent me below for a wrap. She looked past me rather than at me, gave me her orders quietly but briefly, and did not even take the trouble to ignore me. And yet, once or twice, I had found her eyes fixed on me with a cool, half-amused expression, as if she found something in my struggles to carry trays as if I had been accustomed to them, or to handle a mop as a mop should be handled and not like a hockey stick — something infinitely entertaining and not a little absurd.

But that morning, after they had settled to bridge, she followed me to the rail, out of earshot. I straightened and took off my cap, and she stood looking at me, unsmiling.

"Unclench your hands!" she said.

"I beg your pardon!" I straightened out my fingers, conscious for the first time of my clenched fists, and even opened and closed them once or twice to prove their relaxation.

"That's better. Now — won't you try to remember that I am responsible for your being here, and be careful?

"Then take me away from here and put me with the crew. I am stronger now. Ask the captain to give me a man's work. This — this is a housemaid's occupation."

"We prefer to have you here," she

said coldly; and then, evidently repenting her manner: "We need a man here, Leslie. Better stay. Are you comfortable in the forecastle?"

"Yes, Miss Lee."

"And the food is all right?"

"The cook says I am eating two men's rations."

She turned to leave, smiling. It was the first time she had thrown even a fleeting smile my way, and it went to my head.

"And Williams? I am to submit to his bullying?"

She stopped and turned, and the smile faded.

"The next time," she said, "you are to *drop* him!"

But during the remainder of the day she neither spoke to me nor looked, as far as I could tell, in my direction. She flirted openly with Vail, rather, I thought, to the discomfort of Mrs. Johns, who had appropriated him to herself — sang to him in the cabin, and in the long hour before dinner, when the others were dressing, walked the deck with him, talking earnestly. They looked well together, and I believe he was in love with her. Poor Vail!

Turner had gone below, grimly good-humored, to dress for dinner; and I went aft to chat, as I often did, with the steersman. On this occasion it happened to be Charlie Jones. Jones was not his name so far as I know. It was some inordinately long and different German inheritance, and so, with the facility of the average crew, he had been called Jones. He was a benevolent little man, highly religious, and something of a philosopher. And because I could understand German, and even essay it in a limited way, he was fond of me.

"Setz du dich," he said, and moved over so that I could sit on the grating on which he stood. "The sky is fine tonight. *Wunderschön!"*

"It always looks good to me," I observed, filling my pipe and passing my tobacco-bag to him. "I may have my doubts now and then on land, Charlie; but here, between the sky and the sea, I'm a believer, right enough."

"In the beginning He created the heaven and the earth," said Charlie reverently.

We were silent for a time. The ship rolled easily; now and then she dipped her bowsprit with a soft swish of spray; a school of dolphins played astern, and the last of the land birds that had followed us out flew in circles around the masts.

"Sometimes," said Charlie Jones, "I think the Good Man should have left it the way it was after the flood — just sky and water. What's the land, anyhow? Noise and confusion, wickedness and crime, robbing the widow and the orphan, eat or be et."

"Well," I argued, "the sea's that way. What are those fish out there flying for, but to get out of the way of bigger fish?"

Charlie Jones surveyed me over his pipe.

"True enough, youngster," he said; "but the Lord's given 'em wings to fly with. He ain't been so careful with the widow and the orphan."

31

This statement being incontrovertible, I let the argument lapse, and sat quiet, luxuriating in the warmth, in the fresh breeze, in the feeling of bodily well-being that came with my returning strength. I got up and stretched, and my eyes fell on the small window of the chart-room.

The door into the main cabin beyond was open. It was dark with the summer twilight, except for the four rose-shaded candles on the table, now laid for dinner. A curious effect it had — the white cloth and gleaming pink an island of cheer in a twilight sea; and to and from this rosy island, making short excursions, advancing, retreating, disappearing at times, the oval white ship that was Williams's shirt bosom.

Charlie Jones, bending to the right and raised to my own height by the grating on which he stood, looked over my shoulder. Dinner was about to be served. The women had come out. The table-lamps threw their rosy glow over white necks and uncovered arms, and revealed, higher in the shadows, the faces of the men, smug, clean-shaven, assured, rather heavy.

I had been the guest of honor on a steam-yacht a year or two before, after a game. There had been pink lights on the table, I remembered, and the place-cards at dinner the first night out had been caricatures of me in fighting trim. There had been a girl, too. For the three days of that week-end cruise I had been mad about her; before that first dinner, when I had known her two hours, I had kissed her hand and told her I loved her!

Vail and Miss Lee had left the others and come into the chart-room. As Charlie Jones and I looked, he bent over and kissed her hand.

The sun had gone down. My pipe was empty, and from the galley, forward, came the odor of the forecastle supper. Charlie was coughing, a racking paroxysm that shook his wiry body. He leaned over and caught my shoulder as I was moving away.

"New paint and new canvas don't make a new ship," he said, choking back the cough. "She's still the old

Ella, the she-devil of the Turner line. Pink lights below, and not a rat in the hold! They left her before we sailed, boy. Every rope was crawling with 'em.''

> *"The very rats*
> *Instinctively had left it,"* —

I quoted. But Charlie, clutching the wheel, was coughing again, and cursing breathlessly as he coughed.

Chapter 4

I Receive a Warning

The odor of formaldehyde in the forecastle having abated, permission for the crew to sleep on deck had been withdrawn. But the weather as we turned south had grown insufferably hot. The reek of the forecastle sickened me — the odor of fresh paint, hardly dry, of musty clothing and sweaty bodies.

I asked Singleton, the first mate, for permission to sleep on deck, and was refused. I went down, obediently enough, to be driven back with nausea. And so, watching my chance, I waited until the first mate, on watch, disappeared into the forward cabin to eat the night lunch always prepared by the cook and left there. Then, with a blanket and pillow, I crawled into the starboard lifeboat, and settled myself for the night.

35

The lookout saw me, but gave no sign.

It was not a bad berth. As the ship listed, the stars seemed to sway above me, and my last recollection was of the Great Dipper, performing dignified gyrations in the sky.

I was aroused by one of the two lookouts, a young fellow named Burns. He was standing below, rapping on the side of the boat with his knuckles. I sat up and peered over at him, and was conscious for the first time that the weather had changed. A fine rain was falling; my hair and shirt were wet.

''Something doing in the chartroom,'' he said cautiously. ''Thought you might not want to miss it.''

He was in his bare feet, as was I. Together we hurried to the after house. The steersman, in oilskins, was at his post, but was peering through the barred window into the chart-room, which was brilliantly lighted. He stepped aside somewhat to let us look in. The loud and furious voices which had guided us had quieted, but the situation had not relaxed.

Singleton, the first mate, and Turner were sitting at a table littered with bottles and glasses, and standing over them, white with fury, was Captain Richardson. In the doorway to the main cabin, dressed in pajamas and a bathrobe, Vail was watching the scene.

"I told you last night, Mr. Turner," the captain said, banging the table with his fist, "I won't have you interfering with my officers, or with my ship. That man's on duty, and he's drunk."

"Your ship!" Turner sneered thickly. "It's my ship, and I — I discharge you."

He got to his feet, holding to the table. "Mr. Singleton — *hic* — from now on you're — captain. Captain Singleton! How — how d'ye like it?"

Mr. Vail came forward, the only cool one of the four.

"Don't be a fool, Marsh," he protested. "Come to bed. The captain's right."

Turner turned his pale-blue eyes on Vail, and they were as full of danger as a snake's. "You go to hell!" he said.

"Singleton, you're the captain, d'ye hear? If Rich — if Richardson gets funny, put him — in irons."

Singleton stood up, with a sort of swagger. He was less intoxicated than Turner, but ugly enough. He faced the captain with a leer.

"Sorry, old fellow," he said. "but you heard what Turner said!"

The captain drew a deep breath. Then, without any warning, he leaned across the table and shot out his clenched fist. It took the mate on the point of the chin, and he folded up in a heap on the floor.

"Good old boy!" muttered Burns, beside me. "Good old boy!"

Turner picked up a bottle from the table, and made the same unco-ordinated pass with it at the captain as he had at me the morning before with his magazine. The captain did not move. He was a big man, and he folded his arms with their hairy wrists across his chest.

"Mr. Turner," he said, "while we are on the sea I am in command here. You know that well enough. You are drunk tonight; in the morning you will be sober, and I want you to remember what I am going to say. If you — interfere again — with — me — or — my — officers — I — shall — put — you — in — irons.''

He started for the after companionway, and Burns and I hurried forward out of his way, Burns to the lookout, I to make the round of the after house and bring up, safe from detection, by the wheel again. The mate was in a chair, looking sick and dazed, and Turner and Vail were confronting each other.

''You know that is a lie,'' Vail was saying. ''She is faithful to you, as far as I know, although I'm damned if I know why.'' He turned to the mate roughly: ''Better get out in the air.''

Once again I left my window to avoid discovery. The mate, walking slowly, made his way up the companionway to the rail. The man at the wheel reported in the forecastle, when he came down at the end of his watch, that Singleton had seemed dazed, and had stood leaning against the rail for some time, occasionally cursing to himself; that the second mate had come on deck, and had sent him to bed; and that the captain was shut in his cabin with the light going.

There was much discussion of the incident among the crew. Sympathy was with the captain, and there was a general feeling that the end had not come. Charlie Jones, reading his Bible on the edge of his bunk, voiced the general belief.

''Knowin' the Turners, hull and mast,'' he said, ''and having sailed with Captain Richardson off and on for ten years, the chances is good of our having a hell of a time. It ain't natural, anyhow, this voyage with no rats in the hold, and all the insects killed with this here formaldehyde, and ice-cream sent to the fo'c'sle on Sundays!''

But at first the thing seemed smoothed over. It is true that the captain did not speak to the first mate except when compelled to, and that Turner and the captain ignored each other elaborately. The cruise went on without event. There was no attempt on Turner's part to carry out his threat of the night before; nor did he, as the crew had prophesied, order the *Ella* into the nearest port. He kept much to himself, spending whole days below, with Williams carrying him highballs, always appearing at dinner, however, sodden of face but immaculately dressed, and eating little or nothing.

A week went by in this fashion, luring us all to security. I was still lean but fairly strong again. Vail, left to himself or to the women of the party,took to talking with me now and then. I thought he was uneasy. More than once he expressed a regret that he had taken the cruise, laying his discontent to the long inaction. But the real reason was Turner's jealousy of him, the obsession of the dipsomaniac. I knew it, and Vail knew that I knew.

On the 8th we encountered bad weather, the first wind of the cruise. All hands were required for tacking, and I was stationed on the forecastle-head with one other man. Williams, the butler, succumbed to the weather, and at five o'clock Miss Lee made her way forward through the driving rain, and asked me if I could take his place.

"If the captain needs you, we can manage," she said.

"We have Henrietta and Karen, the two maids. But Mr. Turner prefers a man to serve."

I said that I was probably not so useful that I could not be spared, and that I would try. Vail's suggestion had come back to me, and this was my chance to get Williams's keys. Miss Lee having spoken to the captain, I was relieved from duty, and went aft with her. What with the plunging of the vessel and the slippery decks, she almost fell twice, and each time I caught her.

The second time, she wrenched her ankle, and stood for a moment holding to the rail, while I waited beside her. She wore a heavy ulster of some rough material, and a small soft hat of the same material, pulled over her ears. Her soft hair lay wet across her forehead.

"How are you liking the sea, Leslie?" she said, after she had tested her ankle and found the damage inconsiderable.

"Very much, Miss Lee."

"Do you intend to remain a — a sailor?"

"I am not a sailor. I am a deck-steward, and I am about to become a butler."

"That was our agreement," she flashed at me.

"Certainly. And to know that I intend to fulfill it to the letter, I have only to show this."

It had been one of McWhirter's inspirations, on learning how I had been engaged, the small book called *The Perfect Butler*. I took it from the pocket of my flannel shirt, under my oilskins, and held it out to her.

"I have not got very far," I said humbly. "It's not inspiring reading. I've got the wine-glasses straightened out, but it seems a lot of fuss about nothing. Wine is wine, isn't it? What difference, after all, does a hollow stem or green glass make —"

The rain was beating down on us. *The Perfect Butler* was weeping tears, as its chart of choice vintages was mixed with water. Miss Lee looked up, smiling, from the book.

"You prefer *'a jug* of wine,' " she said.

"Old Omar had the right idea; only I imagine, literally, it was a skin of wine. They didn't have jugs, did they?"

"You know the *Rubaiyat?*" she asked slowly.

"I know the jug of wine and loaf of bread part," I admitted, irritated at the slip. "In my home city they're using it to advertise a particular sort of bread. You know — 'A book of verses underneath the bough, a loaf of Wiggins's home-made bread, and thou.' "

In spite of myself, in spite of the absurd verse, of the pouring rain, of the fact that I was shortly to place her dinner before her in the capacity of upper servant, I thrilled to the last two words.

" *'And thou,'* " I repeated.

She looked up at me, startled, and for a second our glances held. The next moment she was gone, and I was alone on a rain-swept deck, cursing my folly.

That night, in a white linen coat, I served dinner in the after house. The meal was unusually gay, rendered so by the pitching of the boat and the uncertainty of the dishes. In the general hilarity, my awkwardness went unnoticed. Miss Lee, sitting beside Vail, devoted herself to him. Mrs. Johns, young and blonde, tried to interest Turner, and, failing in that, took to watching me, to my discomfiture. Mrs. Turner, with apprehensive eyes on her husband, ate little and drank nothing.

Dinner over in the main cabin, they lounged into the chart-room — except Mrs. Johns, who, following them to the door, closed it behind them and came back. She held a lighted cigarette, and she stood just outside the zone of candlelight, watching me through narrowed eyes.

''You got along very well tonight,'' she observed. ''Are you quite strong again?''

''Quite strong, Mrs. Johns.''

"You have never done this sort of thing before, have you?"

"Butler's work? No; but it is rather simple."

"I thought perhaps you had," she said. "I seem to recall you, vaguely — that is, I seem to remember a crowd of people, and a noise — I dare say I did see you in a crowd somewhere. You know, you are rather an unforgettable type."

I was nonplused as to how a butler would reply to such a statement, and took refuge in no reply at all. As it happened, none was needed. The ship gave a terrific roll at that moment, and I just saved the chartreuse as it was leaving the table. Mrs. Johns was holding to a chair.

"Well caught," she smiled, and, taking a fresh cigarette, she bent over a table-lamp and lighted it herself. All the time her eyes were on me, I felt that she was studying me over her cigarette, with something in view.

"Is it still raining?"

"Yes, Mrs. Johns."

"Will you get a wrap from Karen and bring it to me on deck? I — I want air tonight."

The forward companionway led down into the main cabin. She moved toward it, her pale-green gown fading into the shadow. At the foot of the steps she turned and looked back at me. I had been stupid enough, but I knew then that she had something to say to me, something that she would not trust to the cabin walls. I got the wrap.

She was sitting in a deck-chair when I found her, on the lee side of the after house, a position carefully chosen, with only the storeroom windows behind. I gave her the wrap, and she flung it over her without rising.

"Sit down, Leslie," she said, pointing to the chair beside her. And, as I hesitated, "Don't be silly, boy. Elsa Lee and her sister may be as blind as they like. You are not a sailor, or a butler, either. I don't care what you are: I'm not going to ask any questions. Sit down; I have to talk to someone."

I sat on the edge of the chair,

somewhat uneasy, to tell the truth. The crew were about on a night like that, and at any moment Elsa Lee might avail herself of the dummy hand, as she sometimes did, and run up for a breath of air or a glimpse of the sea.

"Just now, Mrs. Johns," I said, "I am one of the crew of the *Ella,* and if I am seen here —"

"Oh, fudge!" she retorted impatiently. "My reputation isn't going to be hurt, and the man's never is. Leslie, I am frightened — you know what I mean."

"Turner?"

"Yes."

"You mean — with the captain?"

"With anyone who happens to be near. He is dangerous. It is Vail now. He thinks Mr. Vail is in love with his wife. The fact is that Vail — well, never mind about that. The point is this: This afternoon he had a dispute with Williams, and knocked him down. The other women don't know it. Vail told me. We have given out that Williams is seasick. It will be Vail next, and, if he puts a hand on him, Vail will kill him; I know him.''

''We could stop this drinking''

''And have him shoot up the ship! I have been thinking all evening, and only one thing occurs to me. We are five women and two men, and Vail refuses to be alarmed. I want you to sleep in the after house. Isn't there a storeroom where you could put a cot?''

''Yes,'' I agreed, ''and I'll do it, of course, if you are uneasy, but I really think —''

''Never mind what you really think. I haven't slept for three nights, and I'm showing it.'' She made a motion to rise, and I helped her up. She was a tall woman, and before I knew it she had put both her hands on my shoulders.

''You are a poor butler, and an indifferent sailor, I believe,'' she said, ''but you are rather a dear. Thank you.''

She left me, alternately uplifted and sheepish. But that night I took a blanket and a pillow into the storeroom, and spread my six feet of length along the greatest diameter of a four-by-seven pantry.

And that night, also, between six and seven bells, with the storm subsided and only a moderate sea, Schwartz, the second mate, went overboard — went without a cry, without a sound.

Singleton, relieving him at four o'clock, found his cap lying near starboard, just forward of the after house. The helmsman and the two men in the lookout reported no sound of a struggle. The lookout had seen the light of his cigar on the forecastle-head at six bells (three o'clock). At seven bells he had walked back to the helmsman and commented cheerfully on the break in the weather. That was the last seen of him.

The alarm was raised when Singleton went on watch at four o'clock. The *Ella* was heaved to and the lee boat lowered. At the same time life-buoys were thrown out, and patent lights. But the early summer dawn revealed a calm ocean, and no sign of the missing mate.

At ten o'clock the order was reluctantly given to go on.

Chapter 5

A Terrible Night

With the disappearance of Schwartz, the *Ella* was short-handed. I believe Captain Richardson made an attempt to secure me to take the place of Burns, now moved up into Schwartz's position. But the attempt met with a surly refusal from Turner.

The crew was plainly nervous and irritable. Sailors are simple-minded men, as a rule; their mental processes are elemental. They began to mutter that the devil-ship of the Turner line was at her tricks again.

That afternoon, going into the forecastle for some of my clothing, I found a curious group. Gathered about the table were Tom, the mulatto cook, a Swede named Oleson, Adams, and Burns of the crew. At the head of the

51

table Charlie Jones was reading the service for the burial of the dead at sea. The men were standing, bareheaded. I took off my cap and stood, just inside the door, until the simple service was over. I was strongly moved.

Schwartz disappeared in the early morning of August 9. And now I come, not without misgiving, to the night of August 12. I am wondering if, after all, I have made clear the picture that is before my eyes: the languid cruise, the slight relaxation of discipline, due to the leisure of a pleasure voyage, the *Ella* again rolling gently, with hardly a dash of spray to show that she was moving, the sun beating down on her white decks and white canvas, on the three women in summer attire, on unending bridge, with its accompaniment of tall glasses filled with ice, on Turner's morose face and Vail's watchful one. In the forecastle, much gossip and not a little fear, and in the forward house, where Captain Richardson and Singleton had their quarters, veiled hostility and sullen silence.

August 12 was Tuesday, a hot August day, with only enough air going to keep our sails filled. At five o'clock I served afternoon tea, and shortly after I went to Williams's cabin in the forward house to dress the wound in his head, a long cut, which was now healing. I passed the captain's cabin, and heard him quarreling with the first mate, who was replying, now and then, sullenly. Only the tones of their voices reached me.

When I finished with Williams, and was returning the quarrel was still going on. Their voices ceased as I passed the door, and there was a crash, as of a chair violently overturned. The next bit I heard.

"Put that down!" the captain roared.

I listened, uncertain whether to break in or not. The next moment, Singleton opened the door and saw me. I went on as if I had heard nothing.

Beyond that, the day was much as other days. Turner ate no dinner that night. He was pale, and twitching; even with my small experience, I knew he was on the verge of delirium tremens.

He did not play cards, and spent much of the evening wandering restlessly about on deck. Mrs. Turner retired early. Mrs. Johns played accompaniments for Vail to sing to, in the chart-room, until something after eleven, when they, too, went to their rooms.

It being impracticable for me to go to my quarters in the storeroom until the after house was settled, I went up on deck. Miss Lee had her arm through Turner's and was talking to him. He seemed to be listening to her; but at last he stopped and freed his arm, not ungently.

"That all sounds very well, Elsa," he said, "but you don't know what you are talking about."

"I know *this*."

"I'm not a fool — or blind."

He lurched down the companionway and into the cabin. I heard her draw a long breath; then she turned and saw me.

"Is that you, Leslie?

"Yes, Miss Lee."

She came toward me, the train of her

soft white gown over her arm, and the light from a lantern setting some jewels on her neck to glittering.

"Mrs. Johns has told me where you are sleeping. You are very good to do it, although I think she is rather absurd."

"I am glad to do anything I can."

"I am sure of that. You are certain you are comfortable there?"

"Perfectly."

"Then — good night. And thank you."

Unexpectedly she put out her hand, and I took it. It was the first time I had touched her, and it went to my head. I bent over her slim cold fingers and kissed them. She drew her breath in sharply in surprise, but as I dropped her hand our eyes met.

"You should not have done that," she said coolly, "I am sorry."

She left me utterly wretched. What a boor she must have thought me, to misconstrue her simple act of kindness! I loathed myself with a hatred that sent me groveling to my blanket in the pantry, and that kept me, once there, awake through all the early part of the summer night.

I wakened with a sense of oppression, of smothering heat. I had struggled slowly back to consciousness, to realize that the door of the pantry was closed, and that I was stewing in the moist heat of the August night. I got up, clad in my shirt and trousers, and felt my way to the door.

The storeroom and pantry of the after house had been built in during the rehabilitation of the boat, and consisted of a short passageway, with drawers for linens on either side, and beyond, lighted by a porthole, the small supply-room in which I had been sleeping.

Along this passageway, then, I groped my way to the door at the end, opening into the main cabin near the chart-room door and across from Mrs. Turner's room. This door I had been in the habit of leaving open, for two purposes — ventilation, and in case I might be, as Mrs. Johns had feared, required in the night.

The door was locked on the outside.

I was a moment or two in grasping the fact. I shook it carefully to see if it had merely caught, and then, incredulous, I put my weight to it. It refused to yield. The silence outside was absolute.

I felt my way back to the window. It was open, but was barred with iron, and, even without that, too small for my shoulders. I listened for the mate. It was still dark, and so not yet time for the watch to change. Singleton would be on duty, and he rarely came aft. There was no sound of footsteps.

I lit a match and examined the lock. It was a simple one, and as my idea now was to free myself without raising an alarm, I decided to unscrew it with my pocket-knife. I was still confused, but inclined to consider my imprisonment a jest, perhaps on the part of Charlie Jones, who tempered his religious fervor with a fondness for practical joking.

I accordingly knelt in front of the lock and opened my knife. I was in darkness and working by touch. I had extracted one screw, and, with a growing sense of satisfaction, was putting it in my pocket before loosening a second, when a board on which I knelt moved under my knee, lifted, as if the other end, beyond the door, had been stepped on. There was no sound, no creak. Merely that ominous lifting under my knee. There was someone just beyond the door.

A moment later the pressure was released. With growing horror of I know not what, I set to work at the second screw, trying to be noiseless, but with hands shaking with excitement. The screw fell out into my palm. In my haste I dropped my knife, and had to grope for it on the floor. It was then that a woman screamed — a low, sobbing cry, broken off almost before it began. I had got my knife by that time, and in desperation I threw myself against the door. It gave way, and I fell full length on the main cabin floor. I was still in darkness. The silence in the cabin was absolute. I could hear the steersman beyond the chart-room scratching a match.

As I got up, six bells struck. It was three o'clock.

Vail's room was next to the pantry, and forward. I felt my way to it, and rapped.

"Vail," I called, "Vail!"

His door was opened an inch or so. I went in and felt my way to his bunk. I could hear him breathing, a stertorous respiration like that of sleep, and yet unlike. The moment I touched him, the sound ceased, and did not commence again. I struck a match and bent over him.

He had been almost cut to pieces with an ax.

Chapter 6

In the After House

The match burnt out, and I dropped it. I remember mechanically extinguishing the glowing end with my heel, and then straightening to such a sense of horror as I have never felt before or since. I groped for the door; I wanted air, space, the freedom from lurking death of the open deck.

I had been sleeping with my revolver beside me on the pantry floor. Somehow or other I got back there and found it. I made an attempt to find the switch for the cabin lights, and, failing, revolver in hand, I ran into the chart-room and up the after companionway. Charlie Jones was at the wheel, and by the light of a lantern I saw that he was bending to the right, peering in at the chart-room window. He turned when he heard me.

"What's wrong?" he asked. "I heard a yell a minute ago. Turner on the rampage?" He saw my revolver then, and, letting go the wheel, threw up both his hands. "Turn that gun, you fool!"

I could hardly speak. I lowered the revolver and gasped. "Call the captain! Vail's been murdered!"

"Good God!" he said. "Who did it?" He had taken the wheel again, and was bringing the ship back to her course. I was turning sick and dizzy, and I clutched at the railing of the companionway.

"I don't know. Where's the captain?"

"The mate's around." He raised his voice. "Mr. Singleton!" he called.

There was no time to lose, I felt. My nausea had left me. I ran forward to where I could dimly see Singleton looking in my direction.

"Singleton! Quick!" I called. "Bring your revolver." He stopped and peered in my direction.

"Who is it?"

"Leslie. Come below, for God's sake!"

He came slowly toward me, and in a dozen words I told him what had happened. I saw then that he had been drinking. He reeled against me, and seemed at a loss to know what to do.

"Get your revolver," I said, "and wake the captain."

He disappeared into the forward house, to come back a moment later with a revolver. I had got a lantern in the meantime, and ran to the forward companionway which led into the main cabin. Singleton followed me.

"Where's the captain?" I asked.

"I didn't call him," Singleton replied, and muttered something unintelligible under his breath.

Swinging the lantern ahead of me, I led the way down the companionway. Something lay huddled at the foot. I had to step over it to get down. Singleton stood above, on the steps. I stooped and held the lantern close, and we both saw that it was the captain, killed as Vail had been. He was fully dressed except for his coat and, as he lay on his back, his cap had been placed over his mutilated face.

I thought I heard something moving behind me in the cabin, and wheeled sharply, holding my revolver leveled. The idea had come to me that the crew had mutinied, and that everyone in the after house had been killed. The idea made me frantic; I thought of the women, of Elsa Lee, and I was ready to kill.

"Where is the light switch?" I demanded of Singleton, who was still on the companion steps, swaying.

"I don't know," he said, and collapsed, sitting huddled just above the captain's body, with his face in his hands.

I saw I need not look to him for help, and I succeeded in turning on the light in the swinging lamp in the center of the cabin. There was no sign of any struggle, and the cabin was empty. I went back to the captain's body, and threw a rug over it. Then I reached over and shook Singleton by the arm.

"Do something!" I raved. "Call the

crew. Get somebody here, you drunken fool!''

He rose and staggered up the companionway, and I ran to Miss Lee's door. It was closed and locked, as were all the others except Vail's and the one I had broken open. I reached Mr. Turner's door last. It was locked, and I got no response to my knock. I remembered that his room and Vail's connected through a bath, and, still holding my revolver leveled, I ran into Vail's room again, this time turning on the light.

A night light was burning in the bathroom, and the door beyond was unlocked. I flung it open and stepped in. Turner was lying on his bed, fully dressed, and at first I thought he too had been murdered. But he was in a drunken stupor. He sat up, dazed, when I shook him by the arm.

''Mr. Turner!'' I cried. ''Try to rouse yourself, man! The captain has been murdered, and Mr. Vail!''

He made an effort to sit up, swayed, and fell back again. His face swollen and purplish, his eyes congested. He made an effort to speak, but failed to be intelligible. I had no time to waste. Somewhere on the *Ella* the murderer was loose. He must be found.

I flung out of Turner's cabin as the crew, gathered from the forecastle and from the decks, crowded down the forward companionway. I ran my eye over them. Every man was there, Singleton below by the captain's body, the crew, silent and horror-struck, grouped on the steps: Clarke, McNamara, Burns, Oleson, and Adams. Behind the crew, Charlie Jones had left the wheel and stood peering down, until sharply ordered back. Williams, with a bandage on his head, and Tom, the cook, were in the group.

I stood, revolver in hand, staring at the men. Among them, I felt sure, was the murderer. But which one? All were equally pale, equally terrified.

"Boys," I said, "Mr. Vail and your captain have been murdered. The murderer must be on the ship — one of ourselves." There was a murmur at that. "Mr. Singleton, I suggest that these men stay together in a body, and that no one be allowed to go below until all have been searched and all weapons taken from them."

Singleton had dropped into a chair, and sat with his face buried in his hands, his back to the captain's body. He looked up without moving, and his face was gray.

"All right," he said. "Do as you like. I'm sick."

He looked sick. Burns, who had taken Schwartz's place as second mate, left the group and came toward me.

"We'd better waken the women," he said. "If you'll tell them, Leslie, I'll take the crew on deck and keep them there."

Singleton seemed dazed, and when Burns spoke of taking the men on deck, he got up dizzily.

"I'm going too," he muttered. "I'll go crazy if I stay down here with *that*."

The rug had been drawn back to show the crew what had happened. I drew it reverently over the body again.

After the men had gone, I knocked at

Mrs. Turner's door. It was some time before she roused; when she answered, her voice was startled.

"What is it?"

"It's Leslie, Mrs. Turner. Will you come to the door?"

"In a moment."

She drew on a dressing-gown, and opened the door.

"What is wrong?"

I told her, as gently as I could. I thought she would faint; but she pulled herself together and looked past me into the cabin.

"That is —?"

"The captain, Mrs. Turner."

"And Mr. Vail?"

"In his cabin."

"Where is Mr. Turner?"

"In his cabin, asleep."

She looked at me strangely, and, leaving the door, went into her sister's room, next. I heard Miss Lee's low cry of horror, and almost immediately the two women came to the doorway.

"Have you seen Mr. Turner?" Miss Lee demanded.

"Just now."

"Has Mrs. Johns been told?"

"Not yet."

She went herself to Mrs. John's cabin, and knocked. She got an immediate answer, and Mrs. Johns, partly dressed, opened the door.

"What's the matter?" she demanded. "The whole crew is tramping outside my windows. I hope we haven't struck an iceberg."

"Adèle, don't faint, please. Something awful has happened."

"Turner! He has killed someone finally!"

"Hush, for Heaven's sake! Wilmer has been murdered. Adèle — and the captain."

Mrs. Johns had less control than the other women. She stood for an instant, with a sort of horrible grin on her face. Then she went down on the floor, full length, with a crash. Elsa Lee knelt beside her and slid a pillow under her head.

"Call the maids, Leslie," she said quietly. "Karen has something for this sort of thing. Tell her to bring it quickly.''

I went the length of the cabin and into the chart-room. The maid's room was here, on the port-side, and thus aft of Mrs. Turner's and Miss Lee's rooms. It had one door only, and two small barred windows, one above each of the two bunks.

I turned on the chart-room lights. At the top of the after companionway the crew had been assembled, and Burns was haranguing them. I knocked at the maids' door, and, finding it unlocked, opened it an inch or so.

''Karen!'' I called — and, receiving no answer: ''Mrs. Sloane!'' (the stewardess).

I opened the door wide and glanced in. Karen Hansen, the maid, was on the floor, dead. The stewardess, in collapse from terror, was in her bunk, uninjured.

Chapter 7

We Find the Ax

I went to the after companionway and called up to the men to send the first mate down; but Burns came instead.

"Singleton's sick," he explained. "He's up there in a corner, with Oleson and McNamara holding him."

"Burns," I said cautiously — "I've found another!"

"God, not one of the women!"

"One of the maids — Karen."

Burns was a young fellow about my own age, and to this point he had stood up well. But he had been having a sort of flirtation with the girl, and I saw him go sick with horror. He wanted to see her, when he had got command of himself; but I would not let him enter the room. He stood outside, while I went in and carried out the stewardess, who was coming to and moaning. I took her forward, and told the three women there what I had found.

Mrs. Johns was better, and I found them all huddled in her room. I put the stewardess on the bed, and locked the door into the next room. Then, after examining the window, I gave Elsa Lee my revolver.

"Don't let anyone in," I said, "I'll put a guard at the two companionways, and we'll let no one down. But — keep the door locked also."

She took the revolver from me, and examined it with the air of one familiar with firearms. Then she looked up at me, her lips as white as her face.

"We are relying on you, Leslie," she said.

And, at her words, the storm of self-contempt and bitterness that I had been holding in abeyance for the last half hour swept over me like a flood. I could have wept for fury.

"Why should you trust me?" I demanded. "I slept through the time when I was needed. And when I wakened and found myself locked in the storeroom, I waited to take the lock off instead of breaking down the door! I ought to jump overboard.''

''We are relying on you,'' she said again, simply; and I heard her fasten the door behind me as I went out.

Dawn was coming as I joined the crew, huddled around the wheel. There were nine men, counting Singleton. But Singleton hardly counted. He was in a state of profound mental and physical collapse. The *Ella* was without an accredited officer, and, for lack of orders to the contrary, the helmsman — McNamara now — was holding her to her course. Burns had taken Schwartz's place as second mate, but the situation was clearly beyond him. Turner's condition was known and frankly discussed. It was clear that, for a time at least, we would have to get along without him.

Charlie Jones, always an influence among the men, voiced the situation as we all stood together in the chill morning air.

"What we want to do, boys" he said, "is to make for the nearest port. This here is a police matter."

"And a hanging matter," someone else put in.

"We've got to remember, boys, that this ain't like a crime on land. We've got the fellow that did it. He's on the boat all right."

There was a stirring among the men, and some of them looked aft to where, guarded by the Swede Oleson, Singleton was sitting, his head in his hands.

"And, what's more," Charlie Jones went on, "I'm for putting Leslie here in charge — for now, anyhow. That's agreeable to you, is it, Burns?"

"But I don't know anything about a ship," I objected. "I'm willing enough, but I'm not competent."

I believe the thing had been discussed before I went up, for McNamara spoke up from the wheel.

"We'll manage that somehow or other, Leslie," he said. "We want somebody to take charge, somebody with a head, that's all. And since you ain't, in a manner of speaking, been one of us, nobody's feelings can't be hurt. Ain't that it, boys?''

"That, and a matter of brains," said Burns.

"But Singleton?" I glanced aft.

"Singleton is going in irons," was the reply I got.

The light was stronger now, and I could see their faces. It was clear that the crew, or a majority of the crew, believed him guilty, and that, as far as Singleton was concerned, my authority did not exist.

"All right," I said. "I'll do the best I can. First of all, I want every man to give up his weapons. Burns!''

"Aye, aye.''

"Go over each man. Leave them their pocket-knives; take everything else.''

The men lined up. The situation was tense, horrible, so that the miscellaneous articles from the pockets — knives, keys, plugs of chewing tobacco, and here and there, among the foreign ones, small combs for beard and mustache — unexpectedly brought to light, caused a smile of pure reaction. Two revolvers from Oleson and McNamara and one nicked razor from Adams completed the list of weapons we found. The crew submitted willingly. They seemed relieved to have someone to direct them, and the alacrity with which they obeyed my orders showed how they were suffering under the strain of inaction.

I went over to Singleton and put my hand on his shoulder.

"I'm sorry, Mr. Singleton," I said, "but I'll have to ask you for your revolver."

Without looking at me, he drew it from his hip pocket and held it out. I took it. It was loaded.

"It's out of order," he said briefly. "If it had been working right, I wouldn't be here."

I reached down and touched his wrist. His pulse was slow and rather faint, his hands cold.

"Is there anything I can do for you?"

"Yes," he snarled. "You can get me a belaying pin and let me at those fools over there. Turner did this, and you know it as well as I do!''

I slid his revolver into my pocket and went back to the men. Counting Williams and the cook and myself, there were nine of us. The cook I counted out, ordering him to go to the galley and prepare breakfast. The eight that were left I divided into two watches, Burns taking one and I the other. On Burns's watch were Clarke, McNamara, and Williams; on mine, Oleson, Adams, and Charie Jones.

It was two bells, or five o'clock. Burns struck the gong sharply as an indication that order, of a sort, had been restored. The rising sun was gleaming on the sails; the gray surface of the sea was ruffling under the morning breeze. From the galley a thin stream of smoke was rising. Some of the horror of the night went with the darkness, but the thought of what waited in the cabin below was on us all.

I suggested another attempt to rouse Mr. Turner, and Burns and Clarke went below. They came back in ten minutes, reporting no change in Turner's condition. There was open grumbling among the men at the situation, but we were helpless. Burns and I decided to go on as if Turner were not on board, until he was in condition to take hold.

We thought it best to bring up the bodies while all the crew was on duty, and then to take up the watches. I arranged to have one man constantly on guard in the after house — a difficult matter where all were under suspicion. Burns suggested Charlie Jones as probably the most reliable, and I gave him the revolver I had taken from Singleton. It was useless, but it made at least a show of authority. The rest of the crew, except Oleson, on guard over the mate, was detailed to assist in carrying up the three bodies. Williams was taken along to get sheets from the linen room.

We brought the captain up first, laying him on a sheet on the deck and folding the edges over him. It was terrible work. Even I, fresh from a medical college, grew nauseated over it. He was heavy. It was slow work, getting him up. Vail we brought up in the sheets from his bunk.

Of the three, he was the most mutilated. The maid Karen showed only one injury, a smashing blow on the head, probably from the head of the ax. For ax it had been, beyond a doubt.

I put Williams to work below to clear away every evidence of what had happened. He went down, ashyfaced, only to rush up again, refusing to stay alone. I sent Clarke with him, and instructed Charlie Jones to keep them there until the cabin was in order.

At three bells the cook brought coffee, and some of the men took it. I tried to swallow, but it choked me.

Burns had served as second mate on a sailing-vessel, and thought he could take us back, at least into more traveled waters. We decided to head back to New York. I got the code-book from the captain's cabin, and we agreed to run up the flag, union down, if any other vessel came in sight. I got the code word for ''Mutiny — need assistance,'' and I asked the mate if he would signal if a vessel came near enough. But he turned sullen and refused to answer.

I find it hard to recall calmly the events of that morning: the three still and shrouded figures prone on deck; the crew, bareheaded, standing around, eyeing each other stealthily, with panic ready to leap free and grip each of them by the throat; the grim determination, the reason for which I did not yet know, to put the first mate in irons; and, over all, the clear sunrise of an August morning on the ocean, rails and decks gleaming, an odor of coffee in the air, the joyous lift and splash of the bowsprit as the *Ella,* headed back on her course, seemed to make for home like a nag for the stable.

Surely none of these men, some weeping, all grieving, could be the fiend who had committed the crimes. One by one, I looked in their faces — at Burns, youngest member of the crew, a blue-eyed, sandy-haired Scot; at Clarke and Adams and Charlie Joines, old in the service of the Turner line; at McNamara, a shrewd little Irishman; at Oleson the Swede. And, in spite of myself, I could not help comparing them with the heavy-shouldered, sodden-faced man below in his cabin, the owner of the ship.

One explanation came to me, and I leaped at it — the possibility of a stowaway hidden in the hold, some maniacal fugitive who had found in the little cargo boat's empty hull ample room to hide. The men, too, seized at the idea. One and all voluntered for what might prove to be a dangerous service.

I chose Charlie Jones and Clarke as being most familiar with the ship, and we went down into the hold. Clarke carried a lantern. Charlie Jones held Singleton's broken revolver. I carried a belaying pin. But, although we searched every foot of space, we found nothing. The formaldehyde with which Turner had fumigated the ship clung here tenaciously, and, mixed with the odors of bilge water and the indescribable heavy smells left by tropical cargoes, made me dizzy and ill.

We were stumbling along, Clarke with the lantern, I next, and Charlie Jones behind, on our way to the ladder again, when I received a stunning blow on the back of the head. I turned dizzy, expecting nothing less than sudden death, when it developed that Jones, having stumbled over a loose plank, had fallen forward, the revolver in his outstretched hand striking my head.

He picked himself up sheepishly, and we went on. But so unnerved was I by this fresh shock that it was a moment or two before I could essay the ladder.

Burns was waiting at the hatchway, peering down. Beside him on the deck lay a blood-stained ax.

Elsa Lee, on hearing the story of Henrietta Sloane, had gone to the maids' cabin, and had found it where it had been flung into the berth of the stewardess.

Chapter 8

The Stewardess's Story

But, after all, the story of Henrietta Sloane only added to the mystery. She told it to me, sitting propped in a chair in Mrs. Johns's room, her face white, her lips dry and twitching. The crew was making such breakfast as they could on deck, and Mr. Turner was still in a stupor in his room across the main cabin. The four women, drawn together in their distress, were huddled in the center of the room, touching hands now and then, as if finding comfort in contact, and reassurance.

"I went to bed early," said the stewardess; "about ten o'clock, I think. Karen had not come down; I wakened when the watch changed. It was hot, and the window from our room to the deck was open. There is a curtain over it, to

82

keep the helmsman from looking in — it is close to the wheel. The bell, striking every half-hour, does not waken me any more, although it did at first. It is just outside the window. But I heard the watch change. I heard eight bells struck, and the lookout man on the forecastle-head call, 'All's well.'

"I sat up and turned on the lights. Karen had not come down, and I was alarmed. She had been — had been flirting a little with one of the sailors, and I had warned her that it would not do. She'd be found out and get into trouble.

"The only way to reach our cabin was through the chart-room, and when I opened the door an inch or two, I saw why Karen had not come down. Mr. Turner and Mr. Singleton were sitting there. They were —" She hesitated.

"Please go on," said Mrs. Turner. "They were drinking?"

"Yes, Mrs. Turner. And Mr. Vail was there, too. He was saying that the captain would come down and there would be more trouble. I shut the door and stood just inside, listening. Mr. Singleton said he hoped the captain would come — that he and Mr. Turner only wanted a chance to get at him.''

Miss Lee leaned forward and searched the stewardess's face with strained eyes.

''You are sure that he mentioned Mr. Turner in that?''

''That was exactly what he said, Miss Lee. The captain came down just then, and ordered Mr. Singleton on deck. I think he went, for I did not hear his voice again. I thought, from the sounds, that Mr. Vail and the captain were trying to get Mr. Turner to his room.''

Mrs. Johns had been sitting back, her eyes shut, holding the bottle of salts to her nose. Now she looked up.

''My dear woman,'' she said, ''are you trying to tell us that we slept through all that?''

''If you did not hear it, you must have slept,'' the stewardess persisted obstinately. ''The door into the main cabin was closed. Karen came down just after. She was frightened. She said the first mate was on deck, in a terrible humor; and that Charlie Jones, who was at the wheel, had appealed to Burns not to leave him there — that trouble was coming. That must have been at half-past twelve. The bell struck as she put out the light. We both went to sleep then, until Mrs. Turner's ringing for Karen roused us.''

''But I did not ring for Karen.''

The woman stared at Mrs. Turner.

''But the bell rang, Mrs. Turner. Karen got up at once and, turning on the light, looked at the clock. 'What do you think of that?' she said. 'Ten minutes to three, and I'd just got to sleep!' I growled about the light, and she put it out, after she had thrown on a wrapper. The room was dark when she opened the door. There was a little light in the chart-room, from the binnacle lantern. The door at the top of the companionway was always closed at night; the light came through the window near the wheel.''

She had kept up very well to this point, telling her story calmly and keeping her voice down. But when she reached the actual killing of the Danish maid, she went to pieces. She took to shivering violently, and her pulse, under my fingers, was small and rapid. I mixed some aromatic spirits with water and gave it to her, and we waited until she could go on.

For the first time, then, I realized that I was clad only in shirt and trousers, with a handkerchief around my head where the accident in the hold had left me with a nasty cut. My bare feet were thrust into down-at-the-heel slippers. I saw Miss Lee's eyes on me, and colored.

"I had forgotten," I said uncomfortably. "I'll have time to find my coat while she is recovering. I have been so occupied —"

"Don't be a fool," Mrs. Johns said brusquely. "No one cares how you look. We only thank Heaven you are alive to look after us. Do you know what we have been doing, locked in down here?

We have been —''

''Please, Adele!'' said Elsa Lee. And Mrs. Johns, shrugging her shoulders, went back to her salts.

The rest of the story we got slowly. Briefly, it was this. Karen, having made her protest at being called at such an hour, had put on a wrapper and pinned up her hair. The light was on. The stewardess said she heard a curious chopping sound in the main cabin, followed by a fall, and called Karen's attention to it. The maid, impatient and drowsy, had said it was probably Mr. Turner falling over something, and that she hoped she would not meet him. Once or twice, when he had been drinking, he had made overtures to her, and she detested him.

The sound outside ceased. It was about five minutes since the bell had rung, and Karen yawned and sat down on the bed. ''I'll let her ring again,'' she said. ''If she gets in the habit of this sort of thing, I'm going to leave.'' The stewardess asked her to put out the light and let her sleep, and Karen did so. The two women were in darkness, and the stewardess dozed, for a minute only. She was awakened by Karen touching her on the shoulder and whispering close to her ear.

"That beast is out there," she said. "I peered out, and I think he is sitting on the companion steps. You listen, and if he tries to stop me I'll call you."

The stewardess was wide awake by that time. She thought perhaps the bell, instead of coming from Mrs. Turner's room, had come from the room adjoining Turner's, where Vail slept, and which had been originally designed for Mrs. Turner. She suggested turning on the light again and looking at the bell register; but Karen objected.

The stewardess sat up in her bed, which was the one under the small window opening on the deck aft. She could not see through the door directly, but a faint light came through the doorway as Karen opened the door.

The girl stood there, looking out. Then suddenly she threw up her hands and screamed, and the next moment there was a blow struck. She staggered back a step or two, and fell into the room. The stewardess saw a white figure in the doorway as the girl fell. Almost instantly something whizzed by her, striking the end of a pillow and bruising her arm. She must have fainted. When she recovered, faint daylight was coming into the room, and the body of the Danish girl was lying as it had fallen.

She tried to get up, and fainted again.

That was her story, and it did not tell us much that we needed to know. She showed me her right arm, which was badly bruised and discolored at the shoulder.

"What do you mean by a white figure?"

"It looked white: it seemed to shine."

"When I went to call you, Mrs. Sloane, the door to your room was closed."

"I saw it close!" she said positively. "I had forgotten that, but now I remember. The ax fell beside me, and I tried to scream, but I could not. I saw the door close, very slowly and without a sound. Then I fainted.''

The thing was quite possible. Owing to the small size of the cabin, and to the fact that it must accommodate two bunks, the door opened *out* into the chart-room. Probably the woman had fainted before I broke the lock of my door and fell into the main cabin. But a *white* figure!

''Karen exclaimed,'' Miss Lee said slowly, ''that someone was sitting on the companion steps?''

''Yes, miss.''

''And she thought that it was Mr. Turner?''

''Yes.'' The stewardess looked quickly at Mrs. Turner, and averted her eyes. ''It may have been all talk, miss, about his — about his bothering her. She was a great one to fancy that men were following her about.''

Miss Lee got up and came to the door where I was standing.

''Surely we need not be prisoners any longer!'' she said in an undertone. ''It is daylight. If I stay here I shall go crazy.''

''The murderer is still on the ship,'' I

protested. "And just now the deck is — hardly a place for women. Wait until this afternoon, Miss Lee. By that time I shall have arranged for a guard for you. Although God knows, with every man under suspicion, where we find any to trust."

"*You* will arrange a guard!"

"The men have asked me to take charge."

"But — I don't understand. The first mate —"

"— is a prisoner of the crew."

"They accuse him!"

"They have to accuse someone. There's a sort of hysteria among the men, and they've fixed on Singleton. They won't hurt him — I'll see to that — and it makes for order."

She considered for a moment. I had time then to see the havoc the night had wrought in her. She was pale, with deep hollows around her eyes. Her hands shook and her mouth drooped wearily. But, although her face was lined with grief, it was not the passionate sorrow of a loving girl. She had not loved Vail, I said to myself. She had not loved Vail! My heart beat faster.

"Will you allow me to leave this room for five minutes?"

"If I may go with you, and if you will come back without protest."

"You are arbitrary!" she said resentfully. "I only wish to speak to Mr. Turner."

"Then — if I may wait at the door."

"I shall not go, under those conditions."

"Miss Lee," I said desperately, "surely you must realize the state of affairs. We must trust no one — *no one*.

Every shadowy corner, every closed door, may hold death in its most terrible form."

"You are right, or course. Will you wait outside? I can dress and be ready in five minutes."

I went into the main cabin, now bright with the morning sun, which streamed down the forward companionway. The door to Vail's room across was open, and Williams, working in nervous haste, was putting it in order. Walking up and down, his shrewd eyes keenly alert. Charlie Jones was on guard, revolver in hand. He came over to me at once.

"Turner is moving, in there," he said, jerking his thunb toward the forward cabin. "What are you going to do? Let a drunken sot like that give us orders, and bang us with a belaying pin when we don't please him?"

"He is the owner. but one thing we can do, Jones. We can keep him from more liquor. Williams!"

He came out, more dead than alive.

"Williams," I said sternly, "I give you an hour to get rid of every ounce of liquor on the *Ella*. Remember, not a bottle is to be saved."

"But Mr. Turner —"

"I'll answer to Mr. Turner. Get it overboard before he gets around. And, Williams!

"Well?" — sullenly.

"I'm going around after you, and if I find so much as a pint, I'll put you in that room you have just left, and lock you in."

He turned even grayer, and went into

the storeroom.

A day later, and the crew would probably have resented what they saw that morning. But that day they only looked up apathetically from their gruesome work of sewing into bags of canvas the sheeted bodies on the deck, while a gray-faced Negro in a white coat flung over the rail cases of fine wines, baskets and boxes full of bottles, dozen after dozen of brandies and liquors, all sinking beyond salvage in the blue Atlantic.

Chapter 9

Prisoners

My first thought had been for the women, and, unluckily, to save them a shock I had all evidences of the crime cleared away as quickly as possible. Stains that might have been of invaluable service in determining the murderer were washed away almost before they were dry. I realize this now, too late. But the ax remained, and I felt that its handle probably contained a record for more skillful eyes than mine to read, prints that under the microscope would reveal the murderer's indentity as clearly as a photograph.

I sent for Burns, who reported that he had locked the ax in the captain's cabin. He gave me the key, which I fastened to a string and hung around my neck under my shirt. He also reported that, as I had suggested, the crew had gone, two at a time, into the forecastle, and had brought up what they needed to stay on deck. The forecastle had been closed and locked in the presence of the crew, and the key given to Burns, who fastened it to his watch-chain. The two hatchways leading to the hold had been fastened down also, and Oleson, who was ship's carpenter, had nailed them fast.

The crew had been instructed to stay aft of the wheel, except when on watch. Thus the helmsman need not be alone. As I have said, the door at the top of the companion steps, near the wheel, was closed and locked, and entrance to the after house was to be gained only by the forward companion. It was the intention of Burns and myself to keep watch here, amidships.

Burns had probably suffered more than any of us. Whatever his relation to the Hansen woman had been, he had been with her only three hours before her death, and she was wearing a ring of his, a silver rope tied in a sailor's knot, when she died. And Burns had been fond of Captain Richardson, in a crew where respect rather than affection toward the chief officer was the rule.

When Burns gave me the key to the captain's room Charlie Jones had reached the other end of the long cabin, and was staring through into the chart-room. It was a time to trust no one, and I assured myself that Jones was not looking before I thrust it into my shirt.

"They're — all ready, Leslie," Burns said, his face working. "What are we going to do with them?"

"We'll have to take them back."

"But we can't do that. It's a two weeks' matter, and in this weather —"

"We will take them back, Burns," I said shortly, and he assented mechanically: —

"Aye, aye, sir."

Just how it was to be done was a difficult thing to decide. Miss Lee had not appeared yet, and the three of us, Jones, Burns, and I, talked it over. Jones suggested that we put them in one of the lifeboats, and nail over it a canvas and tarpaulin cover.

"It ain't my own idea," he said modestly. "I seen it done once, on the *Argentina*. It worked all right for a while, and after a week or so we lowered the jolly-boat and towed it astern."

I shuddered; but the idea was a good one, and I asked Burns to go up and get the boat ready.

"We must let the women up this afternoon," I said, "and, if it is possible, try to keep them from learning where the bodies are. We can rope off a part of the deck for them, and ask them not to leave it."

Miss Lee came out then, and Burns went on deck.

The girl was looking better. The exertion of dressing had brought back her color, and her lips, although firmly set, were not drawn. She stood just outside the door and drew a deep breath.

"You must not keep us prisoners any longer, Leslie," she said. "Put a guard over us, if you must, but let us up in the air."

"This afternoon, Miss Lee," I said.

"This morning you are better below."

She understood me, but she had no conception of the brutality of the crimes, even then.

"I am not a child. I wish to see them. I shall have to testify —"

"You will not see them, Miss Lee."

She stood twisting her handkerchief in her hands. She saw Charlie Jones pacing the length of the cabin, revolver in hand. From the chart-room came the sound of hammering, where the after companion door, already locked, was being additionally secured with strips of wood nailed across.

"I understand," she said finally. "Will you take me to Karen's room?"

I could see no reason for objecting; but so thorough was the panic that had infected us all that I would not allow her in until I preceded her, and had searched in the clothes-closet and under the two bunks. Williams had not reached this room yet, and there was a pool of blood on the floor.

She had a great deal of courage. She glanced at the stain, and looked away again quickly.

"I — think I shall not come in. Will you look at the bell register for me? What bell is registered?"

"Three."

"Three!" she said. "Are you sure?"

I looked again. "It is three."

"Then it was not my sister's bell that rang. It was Mr. Vail's!"

"It must be a mistake. Perhaps the wires —"

"Mrs. Turner's room is number one. Please go back and ask her to ring her bell, while I see how it registers."

But I would not leave her there alone. I went with her to her sister's door, and together we returned to the maids' cabin. Mrs. Turner had rung as we requested, and her bell had registered "One."

"He rang for help!" she cried, and broke down utterly. She dropped into a chair in the chart-room and cried softly, helplessly, while I stood by, unable to think of anything to do or say. I think now that it was the best thing she could have done, though at the time I was alarmed. I ventured, finally, to put my hand on her shoulder.

"Please!" I said.

Charlie Jones came to the door of the chart-room, and retreated with instinctive good taste. She stopped crying after a time, and I knew the exact instant when she realized my touch. I felt her stiffen; without looking up, she drew away from my hand; and I stepped back, hurt and angry — the hurt for her, the anger that I could not remember that I was her hired servant.

When she got up, she did not look at me, nor I at her — at least not consciously. But when, in those days, was I not looking at her, seeing her, even when my eyes were averted, feeling her presence before any ordinary sense told me she was near? The sound of her voice in the early mornings, when I was washing down the deck, had been enough to set my blood pounding in my ears. The last thing I saw at night, when I took myself to the storeroom to sleep, was her door across the main cabin; and in the morning, stumbling out with my pillow and blanket, I gave it a foolish little sign of greeting.

What she would not see the men had seen, and, in their need, they had made me their leader. To her I was Leslie, the common sailor. I registered a vow, that morning, that I would be the common sailor until the end of the voyage.

"Mr. Turner is awake, I believe," I said stiffly.

"Very well."

She turned back into the main cabin; but she paused at the storeroom door.

"It is curious that you heard nothing," she said slowly. "You slept with this door open, didn't you?"

"I was locked in."

She stooped quickly and looked at the lock.

"You broke it open?"

"Partly, at the last. I heard —" I stopped. I did not want to tell her what I had heard. But she knew.

"You heard — Karen, when she screamed?"

"Yes. I was aroused before that — I do not know how — and found I was locked in. I thought it might be a joke

102

—forecastle hands are fond of joking, and they resented my being brought here to sleep. I took out some of the screws with my knife, and — then I broke the door.''

''You saw no one?''

''It was dark; I saw and heard no one.''

''But, surely — the man at the wheel —''

''Hush,'' I warned her; ''he is there. He heard something, but the helmsman cannot leave the wheel.''

She was stooping to the lock again.

''You are sure it was locked?''

''The bolt is still shot.'' I showed her.

''Then — where is the key?''

''The key!''

''Certainly. Find the key, and you will find the man who locked you in.''

''Unless,'' I reminded her, ''it flew out when I broke the lock.''

''In that case, it will be on the floor.''

But an exhaustive search of the cabin floor dicovered no key. Jones, seeing us searching, helped, his revolver in one hand and a lighted match in the other, handling both with an abandon of ease that threatened us alternately with fire and a bullet. But there was no key.

"It stands to reason, miss," he said, when we had given up, "that, since the key isn't here, it isn't on the ship. That there key is a sort of red-hot-give-away. No one is going to carry a thing like that around. Either it's here in this cabin — which it isn't — or it's overboard."

"Very likely, Jones. But I shall ask Mr. Turner to search the men."

She went toward Turner's door, and Jones leaned over me, putting a hand on my arm.

"She's right, boy," he said quickly. "Don't let 'em know what you're after, but go through their pockets. And their shoes!" he called after me. "A key slips into a shoe mighty easy."

But, after all, it was not necessary. The key was to be found, and very soon.

Chapter 10

"That's Mutiny"

Exactly what occurred during Elsa Lee's visit to her brother-in-law's cabin I have never learned. He was sober, I know, and somewhat dazed, with no recollection whatever of the previous night, except a hazy idea that he had quarreled with Richardson.

Jones and I waited outside. He suggested that we have prayers over the bodies when we placed them in the boat, and I agreed to read the burial service from the Episcopal Prayer Book. The voices from Turner's cabin came steadily, Miss Lee's low tones, Turner's heavy bass only now and then. Once I heard her give a startled exclamation, and both Jones and I leaped to the door. But the next moment she was talking again quietly.

Ten minutes — fifteen — passed. I grew restless and took to wandering about the cabin. Mrs. Johns came to the door opposite, and asked to have tea sent down to the stewardess. I called the request up the companionway, unwilling to leave the cabin for a moment. When I came back, Jones was standing at the door of Vail's cabin, looking in. His face was pale.

''Look there!'' he said hoarsely. ''Look at the bell. He must have tried to push the button!''

I stared in. Williams had put the cabin to rights, as nearly as he could. The soaked mattress was gone, and a clean linen sheet was spread over the bunk. Poor Vail's clothing, as he had taken it off the night before, hung on a mahogany stand beside the bed, and above, almost concealed by his coat, was the bell. Jones's eyes were fixed on the darkish smear, over and around the bell, on the white paint.

I measured the height of the bell from the bed. It was well above, and to one side — a smear rather than a print, too indeterminate to be of any value, sinister, cruel.

"He didn't do that, Charlie," I said. "He couldn't have got up to it after — That is the murderer's mark. He leaned there, one hand against the wall, to look down at his work. And, without knowing it, he pressed the button that roused the two women."

He had not heard the story of Henrietta Sloane, and, as we waited, I told him. Some of the tension was relaxing. He tried, in his argumentative German way, to drag me into a discussion as to the foreordination of a death that resulted from an accidental ringing of a bell. But my ears were alert for the voices near by, and soon Miss Lee opened the door.

Turner was sitting on his bunk. He had made an attempt to shave, and had cut his chin severely. He was in a dressing-gown, and was holding a handkerchief to his face; he peered at me over it with red-rimmed eyes.

"This — this is horrible, Leslie," he said. "I can hardly believe it."

"It is true, Mr. Turner."

He took the handkerchief away and looked to see if the bleeding had stopped. I believe he intended to impress us both with his coolness, but it was an unfortunate attempt. His lips, relieved of the pressure, were twitching; his nerveless fingers could hardly refold the handkerchief.

"Wh — why was I not — called at once?" he demanded.

"I notified you. You were — you must have gone to sleep again."

"I don't believe you called me. You're — lying, aren't you?" He got up, steadying himself by the wall, and swaying dizzily to the motion of the ship. "You shut me off down here, and then run things your own damned way." He turned on Miss Lee. "Where's Helen?"

"In her room, Marsh. She has one of her headaches. Please don't disturb her."

"Where's Williams?" He turned to me.

"I can get him for you."

"Tell him to bring me a highball. My mouth's sticky." He ran his tongue over his dry lips. "And — take a message from me to Richardson —" He stopped, startled. Indeed. Miss Lee and I had both started. "To — who's running the boat, anyhow? Singleton?"

"Mr. Singleton is a prisoner in the forward house," I said gravely.

The effect of this was astonishing. He stared at us both, and, finding corroboration in Miss Lee's face, his own took on an instant expression of relief. He dropped to the side of the bed, and his color came slowly back. He even smiled — a crafty grin that was inexpressibly horrible.

"Singleton!" he said. "Why do they — how do they know it was he?"

"He had quarreled with the captain last night, and he was on duty at the time of the — when the thing happened. The man at the wheel claims to have seen him in the chart-room just before, and there was other evidence, I believe. The lookout saw him forward, with something — possibly the ax. Not decisive, of course, but enough to justify putting him in irons. Somebody did it, and the murderer is on board, Mr. Turner.''

His grin had faded, but the crafty look in his pale-blue eyes remained.

''The chart-room was dark. How could the steersman —'' He checked himself abruptly, and looked at us both quickly. ''Where are — they?'' he asked in a different tone.

''On deck.''

''We can't keep them in this weather.''

''We *must*,'' I said. ''We will have to get to the nearest port as quickly as we can, and surrender ourselves and the bodies. This thing will have to be sifted to the bottom, Mr. Turner. The innocent must not suffer for the guilty, and everyone on the ship is under suspicion.''

He fell into a passion at that, insisting that the bodies be buried at once, asserting his ownership of the vessel as his authority, demanding to know what I, a forecastle hand, had to say about it, flinging up and down the small room, showering me with invective and threats, and shoving Miss Lee aside when she laid a calming hand on his arm. The cut on his chin was bleeding again, adding to his wild and sinister expression. He ended by demanding Williams.

I opened the door and called to Charlie Jones to send the butler, and stood by, waiting for the fresh explosion that was coming. Williams shakily confessed that there was no whisky on board.

"Where is it?" Turner thundered.

Williams looked at me. He was in a state of inarticulate fright.

"I ordered it overboard," I said.

Turner whirled on me, incredulity and rage in his face.

"You!"

I put the best face I could on the matter, and eyed him steadily. "There has been too much drinking on this ship," I said. "If you doubt it, go up and look at the three bodies on the deck.

"What have *you* to do about it?" His eyes were narrowed; there was menace in every line of his face.

''With Schwartz gone, Captain Richardson dead, and Singleton in irons, the crew had no officers. They asked me to take charge.''

''So! And you used your authority to meddle with what does not concern you! The ship has an officer while I am on it. And there will be no mutiny.''

He flung into the main cabin, and made for the forward companionway. I stepped back to allow Miss Lee to precede me. She was standing, her back to the dressing-stand, facing the door. She looked at me, and made a helpless gesture with her hands, as if the situation were beyond her. Then I saw her look down. She took a quick step or two toward the door, and, stooping, picked up some small object from almost under my foot. The incident would have passed without notice, had she not, in attempting to wrap it in her handkerchief, dropped it. I saw then that it was a key.

''Let me get it for you,'' I said. To my amazement, she put her foot over it.

"Please see what Mr. Turner is doing," she said. "It is the key to my jewel-case."

"Will you let me see it?"

"No."

"It is not the key to a jewel-case."

"It does not concern you what it is."

"It is the key to the storeroom door."

"You are stronger than I am. You look the brute. You can knock me away and get it."

I knew then, of course, that it was the storeroom key. But I could not take it by force. And so defiantly she faced me, so valiant was every line of her slight figure, that I was ashamed of my impulse to push her aside and take it. I loved her with every inch of my overgrown body, and I did the thing she knew I would do. I bowed and left the cabin. But I had no intention of losing the key. I could not take it by force, but she knew as well as I did what finding it there in Turner's room meant. Turner had locked me in. But I must be able to prove it — my wits against hers, and the advantage mine. I had the women under guard.

I went up on deck.

A curious spectacle revealed itself. Turner, purple with anger, was haranguing the men, who stood amidships, huddled together, but grim and determined withal. Burns, a little apart from the rest, was standing, sullen, his arms folded. As Turner ceased, he took a step forward.

"You are right, Mr. Turner," he said. "It's your ship, and it's up to you to say where she goes and how she goes, sir. But someone will hang for this, Mr. Turner — someone that's on this deck now; and the bodies are going back with us — likewise the ax. There ain't going to be a mistake — the right man is going to swing."

"That's mutiny!"

"Yes, sir," Burns acknowledged, his face paling a little. "I guess you could call it that."

Turner swung on his heel and went below, where Jones, relieved of guard duty by Burns, reported him locked in his room, refusing admission to his wife and Miss Lee, both of whom had knocked on the door.

The trouble with Turner added to the general misery of the situation. Burns got our position at noon with more or less exactness, and the general working of the *Ella* went on well enough. But the situation was indescribable. Men started if a penknife dropped, and swore if a sail flapped. The call of the boatswain's pipe rasped their ears, and the preparation for stowing the bodies in the jolly-boat left them unnerved and sick. Some sort of a meal was cooked, but no one could eat; Williams brought up, untasted, the luncheon he had carried down to the house.

At two o'clock all hands gathered amidships, and the bodies were carried forward to where the boat, lowered in its davits and braced, lay on the deck. It had been lined with canvas and tarpaulin, and a cover of similar material lay ready to be nailed in place. All the men were bareheaded. Many were in tears. Miss Lee came forward with us, and it was from her prayer book that I, too moved for self-consciousness, read the burial-service.

"I am the resurrection and the life," I read huskily.

"The figures at my feet, in their canvas shrouds, rolled gently with the rocking of the ship; the sun beat down on the decks, on the bare heads of the men, on the gilt edges of the prayer book, gleaming in the light, on the last of the land-birds, drooping in the heat on the main cross-trees.

". . . For man walketh in a vain shadow," I read, "and disquieteth himself in vain. . . .

"O spare me a little, that I may recover my strength: before I go hence, and be no more seen."

Chapter 11

"The Deadline"

Mrs. Johns and the stewardess came up late in the afternoon. We had railed off a part of the deck around the forward companionway for them, and none of the crew except the man on guard was allowed inside the ropes. After a consultation, finding the ship very short-handed, and unwilling with the night coming on to trust any of the men, Burns and I decided to take over this duty ourselves, and, by stationing ourselves at the top of the companionway, to combine the duties of officer on watch and guard of the after house. To make the women doubly secure, we had Oleson nail all the windows closed, although they were merely portholes. Jones was no longer on guard below, and I had exchanged

Singleton's worthless revolver for my own serviceable one.

Mrs. Johns, carefully dressed, surveyed the railed-off deck with raised eyebrows.

"For — us?" she asked, looking at me. The men were gathered about the wheel aft, and were out of earshot. Mrs. Sloane had dropped into a steamer-chair, and was lying back with closed eyes.

"Yes, Mrs. Johns."

"Where have you put *them?*"

I pointed to where the jolly-boat, on the port side of the ship, swung on its davits.

"And the mate, Mr. Singleton?"

"He is in the forward house."

"What did you do with the — the weapon?"

"Why do you ask that?"

"Morbid curiosity," she said, with a lightness of tone that rang false to my ears. "And then — naturally, I should like to be sure that it is safely overboard, so it will not be" — she shivered — "used again."

"It is not overboard, Mrs. Johns," I

said gravely. "It is locked in a safe place, where it will remain until the police come to take it."

"You are rather theatrical, aren't you?" she scoffed, and turned away. But a second later she came back to me, and put her hand on my arm. "Tell me where it is," she begged. "You are making a mystery of it, and I detest mysteries."

I saw under her mask of lightness then: she wanted desperately to know where the ax was. Her eyes fell, under my gaze.

"I am sorry. There is no mystery. It is simply locked away for safe-keeping."

She bit her lip.

"Do you know what I think?" she said slowly. "I think you have hypnotized the crew, as you did me — at first. Why has no one remembered that *you* were in the after house last night, that *you* found poor Wilmer Vail, that *you* raised the alarm, that *you* discovered the captain and Karen? Why should I not call the men here and remind them of all that?''

''I do not believe you will. They know I was locked in the storeroom. The door — the lock —''

''You could have locked yourself in.''

''You do not know what you are saying!''

But I had angered her, and she went on cruelly: —

''Who are you, anyhow? You are not a sailor. You came here and were taken on because you told a hardluck story. How do we know that you came from a hospital? Men just out of prison look as you did. Do you know what we called you, the first two days out? We called you Elsa's jail-bird! And now, because you have dominated the crew, we are in your hands!''

''Do Mrs. Turner and Miss Lee think that?''

''They feel as I do. This is a picked crew — men the Turner line has employed for years.''

''You are very brave, Mrs. Johns,'' I said. ''If I were what you think I am, I would be a dangerous enemy.''

"I am not afraid of you."

I thought fast. She was right. It had not occurred to me before, but it swept over me overwhelmingly.

"You are leaving me only one thing to do," I said. "I shall surrender myself to the men at once." I took out my revolver and held it out to her. "This rope is a deadline. The crew know, and you will have no trouble; but you must stand guard here until someone else is sent."

She took the revolver without a word, and, somewhat dazed by this new turn of events, I went aft. The men were gathered there, and I surrendered myself. They listened in silence while I told them the situation. Burns, who had been trying to sleep, sat up and stared at me incredulously.

"It will leave you pretty short-handed, boys," I finished, "but you'd better fasten me up somewhere. But I want to be sure of one thing first: whatever happens, keep the guard for the women."

"We'd like to talk it over, Leslie,"

Burns said, after a word with the others.

I went forward a few feet, taking care to remain where they could see me, and very soon they called me. There had been a dispute, I believe. Adams and McNamara stood off from the others, their faces not unfriendly, but clearly differing from the decision. Charlie Jones, who, by reason of long service and a sort of pious control he had in the forecastle, was generally spokesman for the crew, took a step or two toward me.

"We'll not do it, boy," he said. "We think we know a man when we see one, as well as having occasion to know that you're honest all through. And we're not inclined to set the talk of women against what we think best to do. So you stick to your job, and we're back of you."

In spite of myself, I choked up. I tried to tell them what their loyalty meant to me; but I could only hold out my hand, and, one by one, they came up and shook it solemnly.

"We think," McNamara said, when, last of all, he and Adams came up, "that it would be best, lad, if we put down in the log-book all that has happened last night and today, and this just now, too. It's fresh in our minds now, and it will be something to go by.''

So Burns and I got the log-book from the captain's cabin. The ax was there, where we had placed it earlier in the day, lying on the white cover of the bed. The room was untouched, as the dead men had left it — a collar on the stand, brushes put down hastily, a half-smoked cigar which had burned a long scar on the wood before it had gone out. We went out silently, Burns carrying the book, I locking the door behind us.

Mrs. Johns, sitting near the companionway with the revolver on her knee, looked up and eyed me coolly.

''So they would not do it!''

''I am sorry to disappoint you — they would not.''

She held up my revolver to me, and smiled cynically.

''Remember,'' she said, ''I only said you were a possibility.''

''Thank you; I shall remember.''

By unanimous consent, the task of

putting down what had happened was given to me. I have a copy of the log-book before me now, the one that was used at the trial. The men read it through before they signed it.

August thirteenth.

This morning, between two-thirty and three o'clock, three murders were committed on the yacht *Ella*. At the request of Mrs. Johns, one of the party on board, I had moved to the after house to sleep, putting my blanket and pillow in the store-room and sleeping on the floor there. Mrs. Johns gave, as her reason, a fear of something going wrong, as there was trouble between Mr. Turner and the captain. I slept with a revolver beside me and with the door of the storeroom open.

At some time shortly before three o'clock I wakened with a feeling of suffocation, and found that the door was closed and locked on the outside. I suspected a joke among the crew, and set to work with my pen-knife to unscrew the lock. When I had two screws out, a woman screamed, and I broke down the door.

As the main cabin was dark, I saw no one and could not tell where the cry came from. I ran into Mr. Vail's cabin, next to the storeroom, and called him. His door was standing open. I heard him breathing heavily. Then the breathing stopped. I struck a match, and found him dead. His head had been crushed in with an ax, the left hand cut off, and there were gashes on the right shoulder and the abdomen.

I knew the helmsman would be at the wheel, and ran up the after companionway to him and told him. Then I ran forward and called the first mate, Mr. Singleton, who was on duty. He had been drinking. I asked him to call the captain, but he did not. He got his revolver, and we hurried down the forward companion. The body of the captain was lying at the foot of the steps, his head on the lowest stair. He had been killed like

Mr. Vail. His cap had been placed over his face.

The mate collapsed on the steps. I found the light switch and turned it on. There was no one in the cabin or in the chart-room. I ran to Mr. Turner's room, going through Mr. Vail's and through the bathroom. Mr. Turner was in bed, fully dressed. I could not rouse him. Like the mate, he had been drinking.

The mate had roused the crew, and they gathered in the chart-room. I told them what had happened, and that the murderer must be among us. I suggested that they stay together, and that they submit to being searched for weapons.

They went on deck in a body, and I roused the women and told them. Mrs. Turner asked me to tell the two maids, who slept in a cabin off the chart-room. I found their door unlocked, and, receiving no answer, opened it. Karen Hansen, the lady's-maid, was on the floor, dead, with her skull crushed in. The stewardess, Henrietta

Sloane, was fainting in her bunk. An ax had been hurled through the doorway as the Hansen woman fell, and was found in the stewardess's bunk.

Dawn coming by that time, I suggested a guard at the two companionways, and this was done. The men were searched and all weapons taken from them. Mr. Singleton was under the suspicion, it being known that he had threatened the captain's life, and Oleson, a lookout, claiming to have seen him forward where the ax was kept.

The crew insisted that Singleton be put in irons. He made no objection, and we locked him in his own room in the forward house. Owing to the loss of Schwartz, the second mate, already recorded in this log-book (see entry for August ninth), the death of the captain, and the imprisonment of the first mate, the ship was left without officers. Until Mr. Turner could make an arrangement, the crew nominated Burns, one of themselves, as mate, and asked me to assume command. I protested that I knew nothing of navigation, but agreed on its being represented that, as I was not one of them, there could be no ill feeling.

The ship was searched, on the possibility of finding a stowaway in the hold. But nothing was found. I divided the men into two watches, Burns taking one and I the other. We nailed up the after companionway, and forbade any member of the crew to enter the after house. The forecastle was also locked, the men bringing their belongings on deck. The stewardess recovered and told her story, which, in her own writing, will be added to this record.

The bodies of the dead were brought on deck and sewed into canvas, and later, with appropriate services, placed in the jolly-boat, it being the intention, later on, to tow the boat behind us. Mr. Turner insisted that the bodies be buried at sea, and, on the crew opposing this, retired to his cabin, announcing that he considered the position of the men a mutiny.

Some feeling having arisen among the women of the party that I might know more of the crimes than was generally supposed, having been in the after house at the time they were committed, and having no references, I this afternoon voluntarily surrendered myself to Burns, acting first mate. The men, however, refused to accept this surrender, only two, Adams and McNamara, favoring it. I expect to give myself up to the police at the nearest port, until the matter is thoroughly probed.

The ax is locked in the captain's cabin.

(Signed) RALPH LESLIE.

John Robert Burns
Charles Klineordlinger
(Jones)
William McNamara
Carl L. Clarke
Witnesses   Joseph Q. Adams

John Oleson
Tom MacKenzie
Obadiah Williams

Chapter 12

The First Mate Talks

Williams came up on deck late that afternoon, with a scared face, and announced that Mr. Turner had locked himself in his cabin, and was raving in delirium on the other side of the door. I sent Burns down — having decided, in view of Mrs. John's accusation, to keep away from the living quarters of the family. Burns's report corroborated what Williams had said. Turner was in the grip of delirium tremens, and the *Ella* was without owner or officers.

Turner refused to open either door for us. As well as we could make out, he was moving rapidly but almost noiselessly up and down the room, muttering to himself, now and then throwing himself on the bed, only to get up at once. He rang his bell a dozen times, and summoned Williams, only, in reply to the butler's palpitating knock, to stand beyond the door and refuse to open it or to voice any request. The situation became so urgent that finally I was forced to go down, with no better success.

Mrs. Turner dragged herself across, on the state of affairs being reported to her, and, after two or three abortive attempts, succeeded in getting a reply from him.

"Marsh!" she called. "I want to talk to you. Let me in!"

"They'll get us," he said craftily.

"Us? Who is with you?"

"Vail," he replied promptly. "He's here talking. He won't let me sleep."

"Tell him to give you the key and you will keep it for him so no one can get him," I prompted. I had had some experience with such cases in the hospital.

She tried it without any particular hope, but it succeeded immediately. He pushed the key out under the door, and almost at once we heard him throw himself on the bed, as if satisfied that the problem of his security was solved.

Mrs. Turner held the key out to me, but I would not take it.

"Give it to Williams," I said. "You must understand, Mrs. Turner, that I cannot take it."

She was a woman of few words, and after a glance at my determined face she turned to the butler.

"You will have to look after Mr. Turner, Williams. See that he is comfortable, and try to keep him in bed."

Williams put out a trembling hand, but, before he took the key, Turner's voice rose petulantly on the other side of the door.

"For God's sake, Wilmer," he cried plaintively, "get out and let me sleep! I haven't slept for a month."

Williams gave a whoop of fear, and ran out of the cabin. From that moment, I believe, the after house was the safest spot on the ship. To my knowledge, no member of the crew so much as passed it on the starboard side, where Vail's and Turner's cabins were situated. It was the one good turn the owner of the *Ella* did us on that hideous return journey; for, during most of the sixteen days that it took us to get back, he lay in his cabin, alternating the wild frenzy of delirium tremens with quieter moments when he glared at us with crafty, murderous eyes, and picked incessantly at the bandages that tied him down. Not an instant did he sleep, that we could discover; and always, day or night, Vail was with him, and they were quarreling.

The four women took care of him as best they could. For a time they gave him the bromides I prepared, taking my medical knowledge without question. In the horror of the situation, curiosity had no place, and class distinctions were forgotten. That great leveler, a common trouble, put Henrietta Sloane, the stewardess, and the women of the party at the same table in the after house, where none ate, and placed the responsibility for the ship, although I was nominally in command, on the shoulders of all the men. And there sprang up among them a sort of *esprit de corps,* curious under the circumstances, and partly explained, perhaps by the belief that in imprisoning Singleton they had the murderer safely in hand. What they thought of Turner's possible connection with the crime, I do not know.

Personally, I was convinced that Turner was guilty. Perhaps, lulled into a false security by the incarceration of the two men, we unconsciously relaxed our vigilance. But by the first night the crew were somewhat calmer. Here and there a pipe was lighted, and a plug of tobacco went the rounds. The forecastle supper, served on deck, was eaten; and Charlie Jones, securing a permission that I thought it best to grant, went forward and painted a large black cross on the side of the jolly-boat, and below it the date, August 13, 1911. The crew watched in respectful silence.

The weather was in our favor, the wind on our quarter, a blue sky heaped with white cloud masses, with the sunset fringed with the deepest rose. The *Ella* made no great way, but sailed easily. Burns and I alternated at the forward companionway, and, although the men were divided into watches, the entire crew was on duty virtually all the time.

I find, on consulting the book in which I recorded, beginning with that day, the incidents of the return voyage, that two things happened that evening. One was my interview with Singleton; the other was my curious and depressing clash with Elsa Lee, on the deck that night.

Turner being quiet and Burns on watch at the beginning of the second dog watch, six o'clock, I went forward to the room where Singleton was imprisoned. Burns gave me the key, and advised me to take a weapon. I did not, however, nor was it needed.

The first mate was sitting on the edge of his bunk, in his attitude of the morning, his head in his hands. As I entered, he looked up and nodded. His color was still bad; he looked ill and nervous, as might have been expected after his condition the night before.

"For God's sake, Leslie," he said, "tell them to open the window. I'm choking!"

He was right: the room was stifling. I opened the door behind me, and stood in the doorway, against a rush for freedom. But he did not move. He sank back into his dejected attitude.

"Will you eat some soup, if I send it?"

He shook his head.

"Is there anything you care for?"

"Better let me starve; I'm gone, anyhow."

"Singleton," I said, "I wish you would tell me about last night. If you did it, we've got you. If you didn't, you'd better let me take your own account of what happened, while it's fresh in your mind. Or, better still, write it yourself."

He held out his right hand. I saw that it was shaking violently.

"Couldn't hold a pen," he said tersely. "Wouldn't be believed, anyhow."

The air being somewhat better, I

closed and locked the door again, and, coming in, took out my notebook and pencil. He watched me craftily. ''You can write it,'' he said, ''if you'll give it to me to keep. I'm not going to put the rope around my own neck. If it's all right, my lawyers will use it. If it isn't —'' He shrugged his shoulders.

I had never liked the man, and his tacit acknowledgment that he might incriminate himself made me eye him with shuddering distaste. But I took down his story, and reproduce it here, minus the technicalities and profanity with which it was interlarded.

Briefly, Singleton's watch began at midnight. The captain, who had been complaining of lumbago, had had the cook prepare him a mustard poultice, and had retired early. Burns was on watch from eight to twelve, and, on coming into the forward house at a quarter after eleven o'clock to eat his night lunch, reported to Singleton that the captain was in bed and that Mr. Turner had been asking for him. Singleton, therefore, took his cap and went on deck. This was about twenty minutes after eleven. He had had a drink or two earlier in the evening, and he took another in his cabin when he got his cap.

He found Turner in the chart-room, playing solitaire and drinking. He was alone, and he asked Singleton to join him. The first mate looked at his watch and accepted the invitation, but decided to look around the forward house to be sure the captain was asleep. He went on deck. He could hear Burns and the lookout talking. The forward house was dark. He listened outside the captain's door, and heard him breathing heavily, as if asleep. He stood there for a moment. He had an uneasy feeling that someone was watching him. He thought of Schwartz, and was uncomfortable. He did not feel the whisky at all.

He struck a light and looked around. There was no one in sight. He could hear Charlie Jones in the forecastle drumming on his banjo, and Burns whistling the same tune as he went aft to strike the bell. (It was the duty of the officer on watch to strike the hour.) It was then half after eleven. As he passed the captain's door again, his foot struck something, and it fell to the floor. He was afraid the captain had been roused, and stood still until he heard him breathing regularly again. Then he stooped down. His foot had struck an ax upright against the captain's door, and had knocked it down.

The ax belonged on the outer wall of the forward house. It was a rule that it must not be removed from its place except in emergency, and the first mate carried it out and leaned it against the forward port corner of the after house when he went below. Later, on his watch, he carried it forward and put it where it belonged.

He found Turner waiting on deck, and together they descended to the chart-room. He was none too clear as to what followed. They drank together. Vail tried to get Turner to bed, and failed. He believed that Burns had called the captain. The captain had ordered him to the deck, and there had been a furious quarrel. He felt ill by that time, and, when he went on watch at midnight, Burns was uncertain about leaving him. He was not intoxicated, he maintained, until after half-past one. He was able to strike the bell without difficulty, and spoke each time he went aft, to Charlie Jones, who was at the wheel.

After that, however, he suddenly felt strange. He thought he had been doped, and told the helmsman so. He asked Jones to strike the bell for him, and, going up on the forecastle head, lay down on the boards and fell asleep. He did not awaken until he heard six bells struck — three o'clock. And, before he had fully roused, I had called him.

"Then," I said, "when the lookout saw you with the ax, you were replacing it?"

"Yes."

"The lookout says you were not on deck between two and three o'clock."

"How does he know? I was asleep."

"You had threatened to get the captain."

"I had a revolver; I didn't need to use

an ax."

Much as I disliked the man, I was inclined to believe his story, although I thought he was keeping something back. I leaned forward.

"Singleton," I said, "if you didn't do it — and I want to think you did not — who did?"

He shrugged his shoulders.

"We have women aboard. We ought to know what precautions to take."

"I wasn't the only man on deck that night. Burns was about, and he had a quarrel with the Hansen woman. Jones was at the wheel, too. Why don't you lock up Jones?"

"We are all under suspicion," I admitted. "But you had threatened the captain."

"I never threatened the girl or Mr. Vail."

I had no answer to this, and we both fell silent. Singleton was the first to speak: —

"How are you going to get back? The men can sail a course, but who is to lay it out? Turner? No Turner ever knew anything about a ship but what it made for him.''

''Turner is sick. Look here, Singleton, you want to get back as much as we do, or more. Wouldn't you be willing to lay a course, if you were taken out once a day? Burns is doing it, but he doesn't pretend to know much about it, and — we have the bodies.''

But he turned ugly again, and refused to help unless he was given his freedom, and that I knew the crew would not agree to.

''You'll be sick enough before you get back!'' he snarled.

Chapter 13

The White Light

With the approach of night our vigilance was doubled. There was no thought of sleep among the crew, and, with the twilight, there was a distinct return of the terror of the morning.

Gathered around the wheel, the crew listened while Jones read evening prayer. Between the two houses, where the deck was roped off, Miss Lee was alone, pacing back and forward, her head bent, her arms dropped listlessly.

The wind had gone, and the sails hung loose over our heads. I stood by the port rail. Although my back was toward Miss Lee, I was conscious of her every movement; and so I knew when she stooped under the rope and moved lightly toward the starboard rail.

Quick as she was, I was quicker.

There was still light enough to see her face as she turned when I called to her: —

"Miss Lee! You must not leave the rope."

"*Must* not?"

"I am sorry to seem arbitrary. It is for your own safety."

I was crossing the deck toward her as I spoke. I knew what she was going to do. I believe, when she saw my face, that she read my knowledge in it. She turned back from the rail and faced me.

"Surely I may go to the rail!"

"It would be unwise, if for no other reason than discipline."

"Discipline! Are *you* trying to discipline *me?*"

"Miss Lee, you do not seem to understand," I said, as patiently as I could. "Just now I am in charge of the *Ella*. It does not matter how unfit I am — the fact remains. Nor does it concern me that your brother-in-law owns the ship. I am in charge of it, and, God willing, there will be no more crimes on it. You will go back to the part of the

145

deck that is reserved for you, or you will go below and stay there.''

She flushed with anger, and stood there with her head thrown back, eyeing me with a contempt that cut me to the quick. The next moment she wheeled and, raising her hand, flung toward the rail the key to the storeroom door. I caught her hand — too late.

But fate was on my side, after all. As I stood, still gripping her wrist, the key fell ringing almost at my feet. It had struck one of the lower yard-braces. I stooped, and, picking it up, pocketed it.

She was dazed, I think. She made no effort to free her arm, but she put her other hand to her heart unexpectedly, and I saw that she was profoundly shocked. I led her, unprotesting, to a deck-chair, and put her down in it; and still she had not spoken. She lay back and closed her eyes. She was too strong to faint; she was superbly healthy. But she knew as well as I did what that key meant, and she had delivered it into my hands. As for me, I was driven hard that night; for, as I stood there looking down at her, she held out her hand to me, palm up.

"Please!" she said pleadingly. "What does it mean to you, Leslie? We were kind to you, weren't we? When you were ill, we took you on, my sister and I, and now you hate us. Please!"

"Hate you!"

"He didn't know what he was doing. He wasn't sane. No sane man kills — that way. He had a revolver, if he had wanted — *Please* give me that key!"

"Someone will suffer. Would you have the innocent suffer with the guilty?"

"If they cannot prove it against anyone —"

"They may prove it against me."

"You!"

"I was in the after house," I said doggedly. "I was the one to raise an alarm and to find the bodies. You do not know anything about me. I am — 'Elsa's jail-bird'!"

"Who told you that?"

"It does not matter — I know it. I told you the truth, Miss Elsa; I came here from the hospital. But I may have to fight for my life. Against the Turner money and influence, I have only — this key. Shall I give it to you?''

I held it out to her on the palm of my hand. It was melodramatic, probably; but I was very young, and by that time wildly in love with her. I thought, for a moment, that she would take it; but she only drew a deep breath and pushed my hand away.

''Keep it,'' she said. ''I am ashamed.''

We were silent after that, she staring out over the rail at the deepening sky; and, looking at her as one looks at a star, I thought she had forgotten my presence, so long she sat silent. The voices of the men aft died away gradually as, one by one, they rolled themselves in blankets on the deck, not to sleep, but to rest and watch. The lookout, in his lonely perch high above the deck, called down guardedly to ask for company, and one of the crew went up.

When she turned to me again, it was

to find my eyes fixed on her.

"You say you have neither money nor influence. And yet, you are a gentleman."

"I hope so."

"You know what I mean" — impatiently. "You are not a common sailor."

"I did not claim to be one."

"You are quite determined we shall not know anything about you?"

"There is nothing to know. I have given you my name, which is practically all I own in the world. I needed a chance to recover from an illness, and I was obliged to work. This offered the best opportunity to combine both."

"You are not getting much chance to rest," she said, with a sigh, and got up. I went with her to the companionway, and opened the door. She turned and looked at me.

"Good night."

"Good night, Miss Lee."

"I — I feel very safe with you on guard," she said, and held out her hand. I took it in mine, with my heart leaping.

It was as cold as ice.

That night, at four bells, I mustered the crew as silently as possible around the jolly-boat, and we lowered it into the water. The possibility of a dead calm had convinced me that the sooner it was done the better. We arranged to tow the boat astern, and Charlie Jones suggested a white light in its bow, so we could be sure at night that it had not broken loose.

Accordingly, we attached to the bow of the jolly-boat a tailed block with an endless fall riven through it, so as to be able to haul in and refill the lantern. Five bells struck by the time we had arranged the towing-line.

We dropped the jolly-boat astern and made fast the rope. It gave me a curious feeling, that small boat rising and falling behind us, with its dead crew, and its rocking light, and, on its side above the water-line, the black cross — a curious feeling of pursuit, as if, across the water, they in the boat were following us. And, perhaps because the light varied, sometimes it seemed to drop behind, as if wearying of the chase, and again, in great leaps, to be overtaking us, to be almost upon us.

An open boat with a small white light and a black cross on the side.

Chapter 14

From the Crow's Nest

The night passed without incident, except for one thing that we were unable to verify. At six bells, during the darkest hour of the night that precedes the early dawn of summer, Adams, from the crow's nest, called down, in a panic, that there was something crawling on all fours on the deck below him.

Burns, on watch at the companionway, ran forward with his revolver, and narrowly escaped being brained — Adams at that moment flinging down a marlinespike that he had carried aloft with him.

I heard the crash and joined Burns, and together we went over the deck and both houses. Everything was quiet: the crew in various attitudes of exhausted sleep, their chests and ditty-bags around them; Oleson at the wheel; and Singleton in his jail-room, breathing heavily.

Adams's nerve was completely gone, and, being now thoroughly awake, I joined him in the crow's nest. Nothing could convince him that he had been the victim of a nervous hallucination. He stuck to his story firmly.

"It was on the forecastle-head first," he maintained. "I saw it gleaming."

"Gleaming?"

"Sort of shining," he explained. "It came up over the rail, and at first it stood up tall, like a white post."

"You didn't say before that it was white."

"It was shining," he said slowly, trying to put his idea into words. "Maybe not exactly white, but light-colored. It stood still for so long, I thought I must be mistaken — that it was a light on the rigging. Then I got to thinking that there wasn't no place for a light to come from just there."

That was true enough.

"First it was as tall as a man, or taller maybe," he went on. "Then it seemed about half that high and still in the same place. Then it got lower still, and it took to crawling along on its belly. It was then I yelled.''

I looked down. The green starboard light threw a light over only a small part of the deck. The red light did no better. The masthead was possibly thirty feet above the hull, and served no illuminating purpose whatever. From the bridge forward the deck was practically dark.

''You yelled, and then what happened?''

His reply was vague — troubled.

''I'm not sure,'' he said slowly. ''It seemed to fade away. The white got smaller — went to nothing, like a cloud blown away in a gale. I flung the spike.''

I accepted the story with outward belief and a mental reservation. But I did not relish the idea of the spike Adams had thrown lying below on deck. No more formidable weapon short of an ax could be devised. I said as much.

''I'm going down for it,'' I said; ''if

you're nervous, you'd better keep it by you. But don't drop it on everything that moves below. You almost got Burns.''

I went down cautiously, and struck a match where Adams had indicated the spike. It was not there. Nor had Burns picked it up. A splintered board had shown where it had struck, and a smaller indentation where it had rebounded; but the marlinespike was gone, and Burns had not seen it. We got a lantern and searched systematically, without result. Burns turned to me a face ghastly in the oil light.

''Somebody has it,'' he said, ''and there will be more murder! Oh, my God, Leslie!''

''When you went back after the alarm, did you count the men?''

''No; Oleson said no one had come forward. They could not have passed without his seeing them. He has the binnacle lantern and two other lights.'

''And no one came from the after house?''

''No one.''

Eight bells rang out sharply. The

watch changed. I took the revolver and Burns's position at the companionway, while Burns went aft. He lined up the men by the binnacle light, and went over them carefully. The marlinespike was not found; but he took from the cook a long meat-knife, and brought both Negro and knife forward to me. The man was almost collapsing with terror. He maintained that he had taken the knife for self-protection, and we let him go with a warning.

Dawn brought me an hour's sleep, the first since my awakening in the storeroom. When I roused, Jones at the wheel had thrown an extra blanket over me, for the morning was cool and a fine rain was falling.

The men were scattered around in attitudes of dejection, one or two of them leaning over the rail, watching the jolly-boat riding easily behind us.

Jones heard me moving, and turned.

''Your friend below must be pretty bad, sir,'' he said. ''Your lady-love has been asking for you. I wouldn't let them wake you.''

"My — what?"

He waxed apologetic at once.

"That's just my foolishness, Leslie," he said. "No disrespect for the lady, I'm sure. If it ain't so, it ain't, and no harm done. If it is so, why, you needn't be ashamed, boy. 'The way of a man with a maid,' says the Book."

"You should have called me, Jones," I said sharply. "And no nonsense of that sort with the men."

He looked hurt, but made no reply beyond touching his cap. And, while I am mentioning that, I may speak of the changed attitude of the men toward me from the time they put me in charge. Whether the deference was to the office rather than the man, or whether in placing me in authority they had merely expressed a general feeling that I was with them rather than of them, I do not know. I am inclined to think the former. The result, in any case, was the same. They deferred to me whenever possible, brought large and small issues alike to me, served me my food alone, against my protestations, and, while navigating the ship on their own reponsibility, took care to come to me for authority for everything.

Before I went below that morning, I suggested that some of the spare canvas be used to erect a shelter on the after deck, and this was done. The rain by that time was driving steadily — a summer rain without wind. The men seemed glad to have occupation, and, from that time on, the tent which they erected over the hatchway aft of the wheel was their living and eating quarters. It added something to their comfort: I was not so certain that it added to their security.

Turner was violent that day. I found all four women awake and dressed, and Mrs. Turner, whose hour it was on duty, in a chair outside the door. The stewardess, her arm in a sling, was making tea over a spirit-lamp, and Elsa was helping her. Mrs. Johns was stretched on a divan, and on the table lay a small revolver.

Clearly, Elsa had told the incident of the key. I felt at once the atmosphere of antagonism. Mrs. Johns watched me coolly from under lowered eyelids. The stewardess openly scowled. And Mrs. Turner rose hastily, and glanced at Mrs. Johns, as if in doubt. Elsa had her back to me, and was busy with the cups.

"I'm afraid you've had a bad night," I said.

"A very bad night," Mrs. Turner replied stiffly.

"Delirium?"

"Very marked. He has talked of a white figure — we cannot quite make it out. It seems to be Wilmer — Mr. Vail."

She had not opened the door, but stood, nervously twisting her fingers, before it.

"The bromides had no effect?"

She glanced helplessly at the others. "None," she said, after a moment.

Elsa Lee wheeled suddenly and glanced scornfully at her sister.

"Why don't you tell him?" she demanded. "Why don't you say you didn't give the bromides?"

"Why not?"

Mrs. Johns raised herself on her elbow and looked at me.

"Why should we?" she asked. "How do we know what you are giving him? You are not friendly to him or to us. We know what you are trying to do — you are trying to save yourself, at any cost. You put a guard at the companionway. You rail off the deck for our safety. You drop the storeroom key in Mr. Turner's cabin, where Elsa will find it, and will be obliged to acknowledge she found it, and then take it from her by force, so you can show it later on and save yourself!"

Elsa turned on her quickly.

"I told you how he got it, Adèle. I tried to throw it —"

"Oh, if you intend to protect him!"

"I am rather bewildered," I said slowly; "but, under the circumstances, I suppose you do not wish me to look after Mr. Turner?"

"We think not" — from Mrs. Turner.

"How will you manage alone?"

Mrs. Johns got up and lounged to the table. She wore a long satin negligee of some sort, draped with lace. It lay around her on the floor in gleaming lines of soft beauty. Her reddish hair was low on her neck, and she held a cigarette, negligently, in her teeth. All the women smoked, Mrs. Johns incessantly.

She laid one hand lightly on the revolver, and flicked the ash from her cigarette with the other.

''We have decided,'' she said insolently, ''that, if the crew may establish a deadline, so may we. Our deadline is the foot of the companionway. One of us will be on watch always. I am an excellent shot.''

''I do not doubt it.'' I faced her. ''I am afraid you will suffer for air; otherwise, the arrangement is good. You relieve me of part of the responsibility for your safety. Tom will bring your food to the steps and leave it there.''

''Thank you.''

''With good luck, two weeks will see us in port, and then —''

''In port! You are taking us back?''

''Why not?''

She picked up the revolver and

examined it absently. Then she glanced at me, and shrugged her shoulders. "How can we know? Perhaps this is a mutiny, and you are on your way to some God-forsaken island. That's the usual thing among pirates, isn't it?"

"I have no answer to that, Mrs. Johns," I said quietly, and turned to where Elsa sat.

"I shall not come back unless you send for me," I said. "But I want you to know that my one object in life from now on is to get you back safely to land; that your safety comes first, and that the vigilance on deck in your interest will not be relaxed."

"Fine words!" the stewardess muttered.

The low mumbling from Turner's room had persisted steadily. Now it rose again in the sharp frenzy that had characterized it through the long night.

"Don't look at me like that, man!" he cried, and then — "He's lost a hand! A hand!"

Mrs. Turner went quickly into the cabin, and the sounds ceased. I looked at Elsa, but she avoided my eyes. I turned heavily and went up the companionway.

Chapter 15

A Knocking in the Hold

It rained heavily all that day. Late in the afternoon we got some wind, and all hands turned out to trim sail. Action was a relief, and the weather suited our disheartened state better than had the pitiless August sun, the glaring white of deck and canvas, and the heat.

The heavy drops splashed and broke on top of the jolly-boat, and, as the wind came up, it rode behind us like a living thing.

Our distress signal hung sodden, too wet to give more than a dejected response to the wind that tugged at it. Late in the afternoon we sighted a large steamer, and when, as darkness came on, she showed no indication of changing her course, Burns and I sent up a rocket and blew the fog-horn steadily.

She altered her course then came toward us, and we ran up our code flags for immediate assistance; but she veered off shortly after, and went on her way. We made no further effort to attract her attention. Burns thought her a passenger steamer for the Bermudas, and, as her way was not ours, she could not have been of much assistance.

One or two of the men were already showing signs of strain. Oleson, the Swede, developed a chill, followed by fever and a mild delirium, and Adams complained of sore throat and nausea. Oleson's illness was genuine enough. Adams I suspected of malingering. He had told the men he would not go up to the crow's nest again without a revolver, and this I would not permit.

Our original crew had numbered nine — with the cook and Williams, eleven. But the two Negroes were not seamen, and were frightened into a state bordering on collapse. Of the men actually useful, there were left only five: Clarke, McNamara, Charlie Jones,

Burns, and myself; and I was a negligible quantity as regarded the working of the ship.

With Burns and myself on guard duty, the burden fell on Clarke, McNamara, and Jones. A suggestion of mine that we release Singleton was instantly vetoed by the men. It was arranged, finally, that Clarke and McNamara take alternate watches at the wheel, and Jones be given the lookout for the night, to be relieved by either Burns or myself.

I watched the weather anxiously. We were too short-handed to manage any sort of a gale; and yet, the urgency of our return made it unwise to shorten canvas too much. It was as well, perhaps, that I had so much to distract my mind from the situation in the after house.

The second of the series of curious incidents that complicated our return voyage occurred that night. I was on watch from eight bells midnight until four in the morning. Jones was in the crow's nest, McNamara at the wheel. I was at the starboard forward corner of the after house, looking over the rail. I thought that I had seen the lights of a steamer.

The rain had ceased, but the night was still very dark. I heard a sort of rapping from the forward house, and took a step toward it, listening. Jones heard it, too, and called down to me, nervously, to see what was wrong.

I called up to him, cautiously, to come down and take my place while I investigated. I thought it was Singleton. When Jones had taken up his position at the companionway, I went forward. The knocking continued, and I traced it to Singleton's cabin. His window was open, being too small for danger, but barred across with strips of wood outside, like those in the after house. But he was at the door, hammering frantically. I called to him through the open window, but the only answer was renewed and louder pounding.

I ran around to his door, and felt for the key, which I carried.

''What is the matter?'' I called.

''Who is it?''

"Leslie."

"For God's sake, open the door!"

I unlocked it and threw it open. He retreated before me, with his hands out, and huddled against the wall beside the window. I struck a match. His face was drawn and distorted, and he held his arm up as if to ward off a blow.

I lighted the lamp, for there were no electric lights in the forward house, and stared at him, amazed. Satisfied that I was really Leslie, he had stooped, and was fumbling under the window. When he straightened, he held something out to me in the palm of his shaking hand. I saw, with surprise, that it was a tobacco-pouch.

"Well?" I demanded.

"It was on the ledge," he said hoarsely. "I put it there myself. All the time I was pounding, I kept saying that, if it was still there, it wasn't true — I'd just fancied it. If the pouch was on the floor, I'd know.

"Know what?"

"It was there," he said, looking over his shoulder. "It's been there three times, looking in — all in white, and grinning at me.''

''A man?''

''It — it hasn't got any face.''

''How could it grin at you if it hasn't any face?'' I demanded impatiently. ''Pull yourself together and tell me what you saw.''

It was some time before he could tell a connected story, and, when he did, I was inclined to suspect that he had heard us talking the night before, had heard Adams's description of the intruder on the forecastlehead, and that, what with drink and terror, he had fancied the rest. And yet, I was not so sure.

''I was asleep, the first time,'' he said. ''I don't know how long ago it was. I woke up cold, with the feeling that something was looking at me. I raised up in bed, and there was a thing at the window. It was looking in.''

''What sort of thing?''

''What I told you — white.''

''A white head?''

"It wasn't a head. For God's sake, Leslie! I can't tell you any more than that. I saw it. That's enough. I saw it three times."

"It isn't enough for me," I said doggedly. "It hadn't any head or face, but it looked in! It's dark out there. How could you see?"

For reply, he leaned over and, turning down the lamp, blew it out. We sat in the smoking darkness, and slowly, out of the thick night, the window outlined itself. I could see it distinctly. But how, white and faceless, had *it* stared in at the window, or reached through the bars, as Singleton declared it had done, and waved a fingerless hand at us?

He was in a state of mental and physical collapse, and begged so pitifully not to be left, that at last I told him I would take him with me, on his promise to remain in a chair until dawn, and to go back without demur. He sat near me, amidships, huddled down among the cushions of one of the wicker chairs, not sleeping, but staring straight out motionless.

With the first light of dawn Burns relieved me, and I went forward with Singleton. He dropped into his bunk, and was asleep almost immediately. Then, inch by inch, I went over the deck for footprints, for any clue to what, under happier circumstances, I should have considered a ghastly hoax. But the deck was slippery and sodden, the rail dripping, and between the davits where the jolly-boat had swung was stretched a line with a shirt of Burns's hung on it, absurdly enough, to dry. Poor Burns, promoted to the dignity of first mate, and trying to dress the part!

Oleson and Adams made no attempt to work that day; indeed, Oleson was not able. As I had promised, the breakfast for the after house was placed on the companion steps by Tom, the cook, whence it was removed by Mrs. Sloane. I saw nothing of either Elsa Lee or Mrs. Johns. Burns was inclined to resent the deadline the women had drawn below, and suggested that, since they were so anxious to take care of themselves, we give up guarding the after house and let them do it. We were short-handed enough, he urged, and, if they were going to take that attitude, let them manage. I did not argue, but my eyes traveled over the rail to where the jolly-boat rose to meet the fresh sea of the morning, and he colored. After that he made no comment.

Singleton awakened before noon, and ate his first meal since the murders. He looked better, and we had a long talk, I outside the window and he within. He held to his story of the night before, but was still vague as to just how the thing looked. Of what it was he seemed to have no doubt. It was the specter of either the captain or Vail; he excluded the woman, because she was shorter. As I stood outside, he measured on me the approximate height of the apparition — somewhere about five feet eight. He could see Burns's shirt, he admitted, but the *thing* had been close to the window.

I found myself convinced against my will, and that afternoon, alone, I made a second and more thorough examination of the forecastle and the hold. In the former I found nothing. Having been closed for over twenty-four hours, it was stifling and full of odors. The crew, abandoning in haste, had left it in disorder. I made a systematic search beginning forward and working back. I prodded in and under bunks, and moved the clothing that hung on every hook and swung, to the undoing of my nerves, with every swell. Much curious salvage I found under mattresses and beneath bunks: a rosary and a dozen filthy pictures under the same pillow; more than one bottle of whisky; and even, where it had been dropped in the haste of flight, a bottle of cocaine. The bottle set me to thinking: had we a dope fiend on board, and, if we had, who was it?

The examination of the hold led to one curious and not easily explained discovery. The *Ella* was in gravel ballast, and my search there was difficult and nerve-racking. The creaking of the girders and floor-plates, the groaning overhead of the trestle-trees, and once an unexpected list that sent me careening, head first, against a ballast-tank, made my position distinctly disagreeable. And above all the incidental noises of a ship's hold was one that I could not place — a regular knocking, which kept time with the list of the boat.

I located it at last, approximately, at one of the ballast ports, but there was nothing to be seen. The port had been carefully barred and calked over. The sound was not loud. Down there among the other noises, I seemed to feel as well as hear it. I sent Burns down, and he came up, puzzled.

"It's outside," he said. "Something cracking against her ribs."

"You didn't notice it yesterday, did you?"

"No; but yesterday we were not listening for noises."

The knocking was on the port side. We went forward together, and, leaning well out, looked over the rail.

The missing marlinespike was swinging there, banging against the hull with every roll of the ship. It was fastened by a rope lanyard to a large bolt below the rail, and fastened with what Burns called a Blackwell hitch — a sailor's knot.

Chapter 16

Jones Stumbles over Something

I find, from my journal, that the next seven days passed without marked incident. Several times during that period we sighted vessels, all outward bound, and once we were within communicating distance of a steam cargo boat on her way to Venezuela. She lay to and sent her first mate over to see what could be done.

He was a slim little man with dark eyes and a small mustache above a cheerful mouth. He listened in silence to my story, and shuddered when I showed him the jolly-boat. But we were only a few days out at that time, and, after all, what could they do? He offered to spare us a hand, if it could be arranged; but, Adams having recovered by that time, we decided to get along as we were. A strange sight we must have presented to the tidy little officer in his uniform and black tie: a haggard, unshaven lot of men, none too clean, all suffering from strain and lack of sleep, with nerves ready to snap; a white yacht, motionless, her sails drooping — for not a breath of air moved — with unpolished brasses and dirty decks; in charge of all, a tall youth, unshaven like the rest, and gaunt from sickness, who hardly knew a nautical phrase, who shook the little officer's hand with a ferocity of welcome that made him change color, and whose uniform consisted of a pair of dirty khaki trousers and a khaki shirt, open at the neck; and behind us, wallowing in the trough of the sea as the *Ella* lay to, the jolly-boat, so miscalled, with its sinister cargo.

The *Buenos Aires* went on, leaving us a bit cheered, perhaps, but none better off, except that she varified our bearings. The after house had taken no notice of the incident. None of the women had appeared, nor did they make any inquiry of the cook when he carried down their dinner that night. As entirely as possible, during the week that had passed, they had kept to themselves. Turner was better, I imagined; but, the few times when Elsa Lee appeared at the companion for a breath of air, I was off duty and missed her. I thought it was by design, and I was desperate for a sight of her.

Mrs. Johns came on deck once or twice while I was there, but she chose to ignore me. The stewardess, however, was not so partisan, and, the day before we met the *Buenos Aires,* she spent a little time on deck, leaning against the rail and watching me with alert black eyes.

"What are you going to do when you get to land, Mr. Captain Leslie?" she asked. "Are you going to put us all in prison?"

"That's as may be," I evaded. She was a pretty little woman, plump and dark, and she slid her hand along the rail until it touched mine. Whereon, I did the thing she was expecting, and put my fingers over hers. She flushed a little, and dimpled.

"You *are* human, aren't you?" she asked archly. "I am not afraid of you."

"No one is, I am sure."

"Silly! Why, they are all afraid of you, down there." She jerked her head toward the after house. "They want to offer you something, but none of them will do it."

"Offer me something?"

She came a little closer, so that her round shoulder touched mine.

"Why not? You need money, I take it. And that's the one thing they have — money."

I began to understand her.

"I see," I said slowly. "They want to bribe me."

She shrugged her shoulders.

"That is a nasty word. They might wish to buy — a key or two that you carry."

"The storeroom key, of course. But what other?"

She looked around — we were alone. A light breeze filled the sails and flicked the end of a scarf she wore against my face.

"The key to the captain's cabin," she said, very low.

That was what they wished to buy: the incriminating key to the storeroom, found on Turner's floor, and access to the ax, with its telltale prints on the handle.

The stewardess saw my face harden, and put her hand on my arm.

"Now I *am* afraid of you!" she cried. "When you look like that!"

"Mrs. Sloane," I said, "I do not know that you were asked to do this — I think not. But if you were, say for me what I am willing to say for myself: I shall tell what I know, and there is not money enough in the world to prevent my telling it straight. The right man is going to be punished, and the key to the storeroom will be given to the police, and to no one else."

"But — the other key?"

"That is not in my keeping."

"I do not believe you!"

"I am sorry," I said shortly. "As a matter of fact, Burns has that."

By the look of triumph in her eyes I knew I had told her what she wanted to know. She went below soon after, and I warned Burns that he would probably be approached in the same way.

"Not that I am afraid," I added. "But — keep the little Sloane woman at a distance. She's quite capable of mesmerizing you with her eyes and robbing you with her hands at the same time."

"I'd rather you'd carry it," he said, "although I'm not afraid of the lady. It's not likely, after —"

He did not finish, but he glanced aft toward the jolly-boat. Poor Burns! I believe he had really cared for the Danish girl. Perhaps I was foolish, but I refused to take the key from him; I felt sure he could be trusted.

The murders had been committed on the early morning of Wednesday, the 13th. It was on the following Tuesday that Mrs. Sloane and I had our little conversation on deck, and on Wednesday we came up with the

Buenos Aires.

It was on Friday, therefore, two days after the cargo steamer had slid over the edge of the ocean, and left us, motionless, a painted ship upon a painted sea, that the incident happened that completed the demoralization of the crew.

For almost a week the lookouts had reported "All's well" in response to the striking of the ship's bell. The hysteria, as Burns and I dubbed it, of the white figure had died away as the men's nerves grew less irritated. Although we had found no absolute explanation of the marlinespike, an obvious one suggested itself. The men, although giving up their weapons without protest, had grumbled somewhat over being left without means of defense. It was entirely possible, we agreed, that the marlinespike had been so disposed, as some seaman's resort in time of need.

The cook, taking down the dinner on Friday evening reported Mr. Turner up and about and partly dressed. The heat was frightful. All day we had had a

182

following breeze, and it had been necessary to lengthen the towing-rope, dropping the jolly-boat well behind us. The men, saying little or nothing, dozed under their canvas; the helmsman drooped at the wheel. Under our feet the boards sent up simmering heat waves, and the brasses were too hot to touch.

At four o'clock Elsa Lee came on deck, and spoke to me for the first time in several days. She started when she saw me, and no wonder. In the frenzied caution of the day after the crimes, I had flung every razor overboard, and the result was as villainous a set of men as I have ever seen.

''Have you been ill again?'' she asked.

I put my hand to my chin. ''Not ill,'' I said; ''merely unshaven.''

''But you are pale, and your eyes are sunk in your head.''

''We are very short-handed and — no one has slept much.''

''Or eaten at all, I imagine,'' she said. ''When do we get in?''

''I can hardly say. With this wind,

perhaps Tuesday.''

''Where?''

''Philadelphia.''

''You intend to turn the yacht over to the police?''

''Yes, Miss Lee.''

''Everyone on it?''

''That is up to the police. They will probably not hold the women. You will be released, I imagine, on your own recognizance.''

''And — Mr. Turner?''

''He will have to take his luck with the rest of us.''

She asked me no further questions, but switched at once to what had brought her on deck.

''The cabin is unbearable,'' she said. ''We are willing to take the risk of opening the after companion door.''

But I could not allow this, and I tried to explain my reasons. The crew were quartered there, for one; for the other, whether they were willing to take the risk or not, I would not open it without placing a guard there, and we had no one to spare for the duty. I suggested that they use the part of the deck reserved for them, where it was fairly cool under the awning; and, after a dispute below, they agreed to this. Turner very weak, came up the few steps slowly, but refused my proffered help. A little later, he called me from the rail and offered me a cigar. The change in him was startling.

We took advantage of their being on deck to open the windows and air the after house. But all were securely locked and barred before they went below again. It was the first time they had all been on deck together since the night of the 11th. It was a different crowd of people that sat there, looking over the rail and speaking in monosyllables: no bridge, no glasses clinking with ice, no elaborate toilets and carefully dressed hair, no flash of jewels, no light laughter following one of poor Vail's sallies.

At ten o'clock they went below, but not until I had quietly located every member of the crew. I had the watch from eight to twelve that night, and at half after ten Mrs. Johns came on deck again. She did not speak to me, but dropped into a steamer-chair and yawned, stretching out her arms. By the light of the companion lantern, I saw that she had put on one of the loose negligees she affected for undress, and her arms were bare except for a fall of lace.

At eight bells (midnight) Burns took my place. Charlie Jones was at the wheel, and McNamara in the crow's nest. Mrs. Johns was dozing in her chair. The yacht was making perhaps four knots, and, far behind the small white light of the jolly-boat showed where she rode.

I slept heavily, and at eight bells I rolled off my blanket and prepared to relieve Burns. I was stiff, weary, unrefreshed. The air was very still and we were hardly moving. I took a pail of water that stood near the rail, and, leaning far out, poured it over my head and shoulders. As I turned, dripping, Jones, relieved of the wheel, touched me on the arm.

"Go back to sleep, boy," he said

kindly. ''We need you, and we're goin' to need you more when we get ashore. You've been talkin' in your sleep till you plumb scared me.''

But I was wide awake by that time, and he had had as little sleep as I had. I refused, and we went forward together, Jones to get coffee, which stood all night on the galley stove.

It was still dark. The dawn, even in the less than four weeks we had been out, came perceptibly later. At the port forward corner of the after house, Jones stumbled over something, and gave a sharp exclamation. The next moment he was on his knees, lighting a match.

Burns lay there on his face, unconscious, and bleeding profusely from a cut on the back of his head — but not dead.

Chapter 17

The Ax Is Gone

My first thought was of the after house. Jones, who had been fond of Burns, was working over him, muttering to himself. I felt his heart, which was beating slowly but regularly, and, convinced that he was not dying, ran down into the after house. The cabin was empty: evidently the guard around the pearl-handled revolver had been given up on the false promise of peace. All the lights were going, however, and the heat was suffocating.

I ran to Miss Lee's door, and tried it. It was locked, but almost instantly she spoke from inside: —

"What is it?"

"Nothing much. Can you come out?"

She came a moment later, and I asked her to call into each cabin to see if everyone was safe. The result was reassuring — no one had been disturbed; and I was put to it to account to Miss Lee for my anxiety without telling her what had happened. I made some sort of excuse, which I have forgotten, except that she evidently did not believe it.

On deck, the men were gathered around Burns. There were ominous faces among them, and mutterings of hatred and revenge; for Burns had been popular — the best-liked man among them all. Jones, wrought to the highest pitch, had even shed a few shamefaced tears, and was obliterating the humiliating memory by an extra brusqueness of manner.

We carried the injured man aft, and with such implements as I had I cleaned and dressed the wound. It needed sewing, and it seemed best to do it before he regained consciousness. Jones and Adams went below to the forecastle, therefore, and brought up my amputating set, which contained, besides its knives, some curved needles and surgical silk, still in good condition.

I opened the case, and before the knives, the long surgeon's knives which were in use before the scalpel superseded them, they fell back, muttering and amazed.

I did not know that Elsa Lee also was watching until, having requested Jones, who had been a sailmaker, to thread the needles, his trembling hands refused their duty. I looked up, searching the group for a competent assistant, and saw the girl. She had dressed, and the light from the lantern beside me on the deck threw into relief her white figure among the dark ones. She came forward as my eyes fell on her.

"Let me try," she said; and, kneeling by the lantern, in a moment she held out the threaded needle. Her hand was quite steady. She made an able assistant, wiping clean the oozing edges of the wound so that I could see to clip the bleeding vessels, and working deftly with the silk and needles to keep me supplied. My old case yielded also a roll or so of bandage. By the time Burns was attempting an unco-ordinated movement or two, the operation was over and the instruments put out of sight.

His condition was good. The men carried him to the tent, where Jones sat beside him, and the other men stood outside, uneasy and watchful, looking in.

The operating case, with its knives, came in for its share of scrutiny, and I felt that an explanation was due to the men. To tell them the truth, I had forgotten all about the case. Perhaps I swaggered just a bit as I went over to wash my hands. It was my first opportunity, and I was young, and the Girl was there.

"I see you looking at my case, boys," I said. "Perhaps I'm a little late explaining, but I guess after what you've seen you'll understand. The case belonged to my grandfather, who was a surgeon. He was in the war. That case was at Gettysburg."

"And because of your Grandfather you brought it on shipboard!" Clarke said nastily.

"No. I'm a cub doctor myself. I'd

been sick, and I needed the sea and a rest.''

They were not so impressed as I had expected — or perhaps they had known all along. Sailors are a secretive lot.

''I'm thinking we'll all be getting a rest soon,'' a voice said. ''What are you going to do with them knives?''

I had an inspiration. ''I'm going to leave that to you men,'' I said. ''You may throw them overboard, if you wish — but, if you do, take out the needles and silk; we may need them.''

There followed a savage but restrained argument among the men. Jones, from the tent, called out irritably: —

''Don't be fools, you fellows. This happened while Leslie was asleep. I'll swear he never moved after he lay down.''

The crew reached a decision shortly after that, and came to me in a body.

''We think,'' Oleson said, ''that we'll lock them in the captain's cabin, with the ax.''

''Very well,'' I said. ''Burns has the key around his neck.''

Clarke, I think it was, went into the tent, and came out again directly.

"There's no key around his neck," he said gruffly.

"It may have slipped around under his back."

"It isn't there at all."

I ran into the tent, where Jones, having exhausted the resources of the injured man's clothing, was searching among the blankets on which he lay. There was no key. I went out to the men again, bewildered. The dawn had come, a pink and rosy dawn that promised another stifling day. It revealed the disarray of the deck — the basins, the old mahogany amputating case with its lock-plate of bone, the stained and reddened towels; and it showed the brooding and overcast faces of the men.

"Isn't it there?" I asked. "Our agreement was for me to carry the key to Singleton's cabin and Burns the captain's."

Miss Lee, by the rail, came forward slowly, and looked up at me.

"Isn't it possible," she said, "that,

knowing where the key was, someone wished to get it, and so —'' She indicated the tent and Burns.

I knew then. How dull I had been, and stupid! The men caught her meaning, too, and we tramped heavily forward, the girl and I leading.

The door into the captain's room was open, and the ax was gone from the bunk. The key, with the cord that Burns had worn around his neck, was in the door, the string torn and pulled as if it had been jerked away from the unconscious man. Later on we verified this by finding on the back of Burns's neck an abraded line two inches or so in length.

It was a strong cord — the kind a sailor pins his faith to, and uses indiscriminately to hold his trousers or his knife.

I ordered a rigid search of the deck, but the ax was gone. Nor was it ever found. It had taken its bloody story many fathoms deep into the old Atlantic, and hidden it, where many crimes have been hidden, in the ooze and slime of the sea-bottom.

That day was memorable for more than the attack on Burns. It marked a complete revolution in my idea of the earlier crimes, and of the criminal.

Two things influenced my change of mental attitude. The attack on Burns was one. I did not believe that Turner had strength enough to fell so vigorous a man, even with the capstan bar which we found lying near by. Nor could he have jerked the broken cord. Mrs. Johns I eliminated for the same reason, of course. I could imagine her getting the key by subtley, wheedling the impressionable young sailor into compliance. But force!

The second reason was the stronger.

Singleton, the mate, had become a tractable and almost amiable prisoner. Like Turner, he was ugly only when he was drinking, and there was not even enough liquor on the *Ella* to revive poor Burns. He spent his days devising, with bits of wire, a ring puzzle that he intended should make his fortune. And I believe he contrived, finally a clever enough bit of foolery. He was anxious to talk, and complained bitterly of loneliness, using every excuse to hold Tom, the cook, when he carried him his meals. He had asked for a Bible, too, and read it now and then.

The morning of Burns's injury, I visited Singleton.

The new outrage, coming at a time when they were slowly recovering confidence, had turned the men surly. The loss of the ax, the handle of which I had told them would, under skillful eyes, reveal the murderer as accurately as a photograph, was a serious blow. Again arose the specter of the innocent suffering for the guilty. They went doggedly about their work, and wherever they gathered there was muttered talk of the white figure. There was grumbling, too, over their lack of weapons for defense.

The cook was a ringleader of he malcontents. Certain utensils were allowed him; but he was compelled at night to lock them in the galley, after either Burns's inspection or mine, and to turn over the key to one of us.

On the morning after the attack, therefore, Tom, carrying Singleton's breakfast to him, told him at length what had occurred in the night, and dilated on his lack of self-defense should an attack be directed toward him.

Singleton promptly offered to make him, out of wire, a key to the galley door, so that he could get what he wanted from it. The cook was to take an impression of the lock. In exchange, Tom was to fetch him, from a hiding-place which Singleton designated in the forward house, a bottle of whisky.

The cook was a shrewd man, and he let Singleton make the key. It was after ten that morning when he brought it to me. I was trying to get the details of his injury from Burns, at the time, in the tent.

"I didn't see or hear anything, Leslie," Burns said feebly. "I don't even remember being hit. I felt there was someone behind me. That was all."

"There had been nothing suspicious earlier in the night?"

He lay thinking. He was still somewhat confused.

"No — I think not. Or — yes, I thought once I saw someone standing by the mainmast — behind it. It wasn't."

"How long was Mrs. Johns on deck?"

"Not long."

"Did she ask you to do something for her?"

Pale as he was, he colored; but he eyed me honestly.

"Yes. Don't ask me any more, Leslie. It had nothing to do with this."

"What did she ask you to do?" I persisted remorselessly.

"I don't want to talk; my head aches."

"Very well. Then I'll tell you what happened after I went off watch. No, I wasn't spying. I know the woman, that's all. She said you looked tired, and wouldn't it be all right if you sat down for a moment and talked to her."

"No; she said she was nervous."

"The same thing — only better. Then she persisted in talking of the crime, and finally she said she would like to see the ax. It wouldn't do any harm. She wouldn't touch it."

He watched me uneasily.

"She didn't either," he said. "I'll swear to that, Leslie. She didn't go near the bunk. She covered her face with her hands, and leaned against the door. I thought she was going to faint."

"Against the door, of course! And got an impression of the key. The door opens in. She could take out the key, press it against a cake of wax or even a cake of soap in her hand, and slip it back into the lock again while you — What were you doing while she was doing all that?"

"She dropped her salts. I picked them up."

"Exactly! Well, the ax is gone."

He started up on his elbow.

"Gone!"

"Thrown overboard, probably. It is not in the cabin."

It was brutal, perhaps; but the situation was all of that. As Burns fell back, colorless, Tom the cook, brought into the tent the wire key that Singleton had made.

That morning I took from inside of Singleton's mattress a bunch of keys, a long steel file, and the leg of one of his chairs, carefully unscrewed and wrapped at the end with wire — a formidable club. One of the keys opened Singleton's door.

That was on Saturday. Early Monday morning we sighted land.

Chapter 18

A Bad Combination

We picked up a pilot outside the Lewes breakwater — a man of few words. I told him only the outlines of our story, and I believe he half discredited me at first. God knows, I was not a creditable object. When I took him aft and showed him the jolly-boat, he realized, at last, that he was face to face with a great tragedy, and paid it the tribute of throwing away his cigar.

He suggested our raising the yellow plague flag; and this we did, with a ready response from the quarantine officer. The quarantine officer came out in a power-boat, and mounted a ladder; and from that moment my command of the *Ella* ceased. Turner, immaculately dressed, pale, distinguished, member of the yacht club and partner in the Turner line, met him at the rail, and conducted him, with a sort of chastened affability, to the cabin.

Exhausted from lack of sleep, terrified with what had gone by and what was yet to come, unshaven and unkempt, the men gathered on the forecastle-head and waited.

The conference below lasted perhaps an hour. At the end of that time the quarantine officer came up and shouted a direction from below, as a result of which the jolly-boat was cut loose, and, towed by the tug, taken to the quarantine station. There was an argument, I believe, between Turner and the officer, as to allowing us to proceed up the river without waiting for the police. Turner prevailed, however, and, from the time we hoisted the yellow flag, we were on our way to the city, a tug panting beside us, urging the broad and comfortable lines of the old cargo boat to a semblance of speed.

The quarantine officer, a dapper little man, remained on the boat, and busied himself officiously, getting the names of the men, peering at Singleton through his barred window, and expressing disappointment at my lack of foresight in having the bloodstains cleared away.

"Every stain is a clue, my man, to the trained eye," he chirruped. "With an ax, too! What a brutal method! Brutal! Where is the ax?"

"Gone," I said patiently. "It was stolen out of the captain's cabin."

He eyed me over his glasses.

"That's very strange," he commented. "No stains, no ax! You fellows have been mighty careful to destroy the evidence, haven't you?"

All that long day we made our deliberate progress up the river. The luggage from the after house was carried up on deck by Adams and Clarke, and stood waiting for the customhouse.

Turner, his hands behind him, paced the deck hour by hour, his heavy face colorless. His wife, dark, repressed, with a look of being always on guard, watched him furtively. Mrs. Johns, dressed in black, talked to the doctor; and, from the notes he made, I knew she was telling the story of the tragedy. And here, there, and everywhere, efficient, normal, and so lovely that it hurt me to look at her, was Elsa.

Williams, the butler, had emerged from his chrysalis of fright, and was ostentatiously looking after the family's comfort. No clearer indication could have been given of the new status of affairs than his changed attitude toward me. He came up to me, early in the afternoon, and demanded that I wash down the deck before the women came up.

I smiled down at him cheerfully.

"Williams," I said, "you are a coward — a mean, white-livered coward. You have skulked in the after house, behind women, when there was man's work to do. If I wash that deck, it will be with you as a mop."

He blustered something about speaking to Mr. Turner and seeing that I did the work I was brought on board to do, and, seeing Turner's eye on us, finished his speech with an ugly epithet. My nerves were strained to the utmost:

lack of sleep and food had done their work. I was no longer in command of the *Ella;* I was a common sailor, ready to vent my spleen through my fists.

I knocked him down with my open hand.

It was a barbarous and a reckless thing to do. He picked himself up and limped away, muttering. Turner had watched the scene with his cold blue eyes, and the little doctor with his near-sighted ones.

"A dangerous man, that!" said the doctor.

"Dangerous and intelligent," replied Turner. "A bad combination!"

It was late that night when the *Ella* anchored in the river at Philadelphia. We were not allowed to land. The police took charge of ship, crew, and passengers. The men slept heavily on deck, except Burns, who developed a slight fever from his injury, and moved about restlessly.

It seemed to me that the vigilance of the officers was exerted largely to prevent an escape from the vessel, and not sufficiently for the safety of those on board. I spoke of this, and a guard was placed at the companionway again. Thus I saw Elsa Lee for the last time until the trial.

She was dressed, as she had been in the afternoon, in a dark cloth suit of some sort, and I did not see her until I had spoken to the officer in charge. She turned, at my voice, and called me to join her where she stood.

"We are back again, Leslie."

"Yes, Miss Lee."

"Back to — what? To live the whole thing over again in a courtroom! If only we could go away, anywhere, and try to forget!"

She had not expected any answer, and I had none ready. I was thinking — Heaven help me — that there were things I would not forget if I could: the lift of her lashes as she looked up at me; few words we had had together, the day she had told me the deck was not clean; the night I had touched her hand with my lips.

"We are to be released, I believe," she said, "on our own — some legal term; I forget it."

"Recognizance, probably."

"Yes. You do not know law as well as medicine?"

"I am sorry — no; and I know very little medicine."

"But you sewed up a wound!"

"As a matter of fact," I admitted, "that was my initial performance, and it is badly done. It — it puckers."

She turned on me a trifle impatiently.

"Why do you make such a secret of your identity?" she demanded. "Is it a pose? Or — have you a reason for concealing it?"

"It is not a pose; and I have nothing to be ashamed of, unless poverty —"

"Of course not. What do you mean by poverty?"

"The common garden variety sort. I have hardly a dollar in the world. As to my identity — if it interests you at all — I graduated in medicine last June. I spent the last of the money that was to educate me in purchasing a dress suit to

207

graduate in, and a supper by way of celebration. The dress suit helped me to my diploma. The supper gave me typhoid.''

''So *that* was it!''

''Not jail, you see.''

''And what are you going to do now?''

I glanced around to where a police officer stood behind us watchfully.

''Now? Why, now I go to jail in earnest.''

''You have been very good to us,'' she said wistfully. ''We have all been strained and nervous. Maybe you have not thought I noticed or — or appreciated what you were doing; but I have, always. You have given all of yourself for us. You have not slept or eaten. And now you are going to be imprisoned. It isn't just!''

I tried to speak lightly, to reassure her.

''Don't be unhappy about *that,*'' I said. ''A nice, safe jail, where one may sleep and eat, and eat and sleep — oh, I shall be very comfortable! And if you wish to make me exceedingly happy, you will see that they let me have a razor.''

But, to my surprise, she buried her face in her arms. I could not believe at first that she was crying. The policeman had wandered across to the other rail, and stood looking out at the city lights, his back to us. I put my hand out to touch her soft hair, then drew it back. I could not take advantage of her sympathy, of the hysterical excitement of that last night on the *Ella*. I put my hands in my pockets, and held them there, clenched, lest, in spite of my will, I reach out to take her in my arms.

Chapter 19

I Take the Stand

And now I come, with some hesitation to the trial. Hesitation, because I relied on McWhirter to keep a record. And McWhirter, from his notes, appears to have been carried away at times by excitement, and either jotted down rows of unintelligible words, or waited until evening and made up his notes, like a woman's expense account, from a memory never noticeable for accuracy.

At dawn, the morning after we anchored, Charlie Jones roused me, grinning.

''Friend of yours over the rail, Leslie,'' he said, ''Wants to take you ashore!''

I knew no one in Philadelphia except the chap who had taken me yachting once, and I felt pretty certain that he would not associate Leslie the football player with Leslie the sailor on the *Ella*. I went reluctantly to the rail, and looked down. Below me, just visible in the river mist of the early morning, was a small boat from which two men were looking up. One was McWhirter!

"Hello, old top," he cried. "Or *is* it you behind that beard?"

"It's I, all right, Mac," I said, somewhat huskily What with seeing him again, his kindly face behind its glasses, the cheerful faith in me which was his contribution to our friendship — even the way he shook his own hand in default of mine — my throat tightened. Here, after all, was home and a friend.

He looked up at the rail, and motioned to a rope that hung there

"Get your stuff and come with us for breakfast," he said. "You look as if you hadn't eaten since you left."

"I'm afraid I can't, Mac."

"They're not going to hold you, are they?"

"For a day or so, yes."

Mac's reply to this was a violent

résumé of the ancestry and present lost condition of the Philadelphia police, ending with a request that I jump over, and let them go to the place he had just designed as their abiding place in eternity. On an officer lounging to the rail and looking down, however, he subsided into a low muttering.

The story of how McWhirter happened to be floating on the bosom of the Delaware River before five o'clock in the morning was a long one — it was months before I got it in full. Briefly, going home from the theater in New York the night before, he had bought an "extra" which had contained a brief account of the *Ella's* return. He seems to have gone into a frenzy of excitement at once. He borrowed a small car — one scornfully designated as a "road louse" — and assembled in it, in wild confusion, one suit of clothes for me, his own and much too small, one hypodermic case, and armful of newspapers with red scareheads, a bottle of brandy, a bottle of digitalis, one police card, and one excited young lawyer, of the same vintage in law that Mac and I were in medicine. At the last moment, fearful that police might not know who I was, he had flung in a scrapbook in which he had pasted — with a glue that was to make his fortune — records of my exploits on the football field!

A dozen miles from Philadelphia the little machine had turned over on a curve, knocking all the law and most of the enthusiasm out of Walters, the legal gentleman, and smashing the brandy-bottle. McWhirter had picked himself up, kicked viciously at the car, and, gathering up his impedimenta, had made the rest of the journey by foot and street-car.

His wrath at finding me a prisoner was unbounded; his scorn at Walters, the attorney, for not confounding the police with law enough to free me, was furious and contemptuous. He picked up the oars in sullen silence, and, leaning on them, called a loud and defiant farewell for the benefit of the officer.

"All right," he said. "An hour or so

won't make much difference. But you'll be free today, all right, all right. And don't let them bluff you, boy. If the police get funny, tackle them and throw 'em overboard, one by one. You can do it.

He made an insulting gesture at the police, picked up his oars, and rowed away into the mist.

But I was not free that day, nor for many days. As I had expected, Turner, his family, Mrs. Johns, and the stewardess were released, after examination. The rest of us were taken to jail — Singleton as a suspect, the others to make sure of their presence at the trial.

The murders took place on the morning of August 13. The Grand Jury met late in September, and found an indictment against Singleton. The trial began on the 16th of November.

The confinement was terrible. Accustomed to regular exercise as I was, I suffered mentally and physically. I heard nothing from Elsa Lee, and I missed McWhirter, who had got his hospital appointment, and who wrote me cheering letters on pages torn from order-books or on prescription blanks. He was in Boston.

He got leave of absence for the trial, and, as I explained, the following notes are his, not mine. The case was tried in the United States Court, before Circuit Judge Willard and District Judge McDowell. The United States was represented by a district attorney and two assistant attorneys. Singleton had retained a clever young lawyer named Goldstein.

I was called first, as having found the bodies.

"Your name?"

"Ralph Leslie."

"Your age?"

"Twenty-four."

"When and where were you born?"

"November 18, 1887, Columbus, Ohio."

"When did you ship on the yacht *Ella?*"

"On July 27."

"When did she sail?"

"July 28."

"Are you a sailor by occupation?"

"No; I am a graduate of a medical college."

"What were your duties on the ship?"

"They were not well defined. I had been ill and was not strong, I was a sort of deck-steward, I suppose. I also served a few meals in the cabin of the after house, when the butler was incapacitated."

"Where were you quartered?"

"In the forecastle, with the crew, until a day or so before the murders. Then I moved into the after house, and slept in a storeroom there."

"Why did you make the change?"

"Mrs. Johns, a guest, asked me to do so. She said she was nervous."

"Who slept in the after house?"

"Mr. and Mrs. Turner, Miss Lee, Mrs. Johns, and Mr. Vail. The stewardess, Mrs. Sloane, and Karen Hansen, a maid, also slept there; but their room opened from the chart-room."

A diagram of the after house was here

submitted to the jury. For the benefit of the reader, I reproduce it roughly. I have made no attempt to do more than to indicate the relative positions of rooms and companionways.

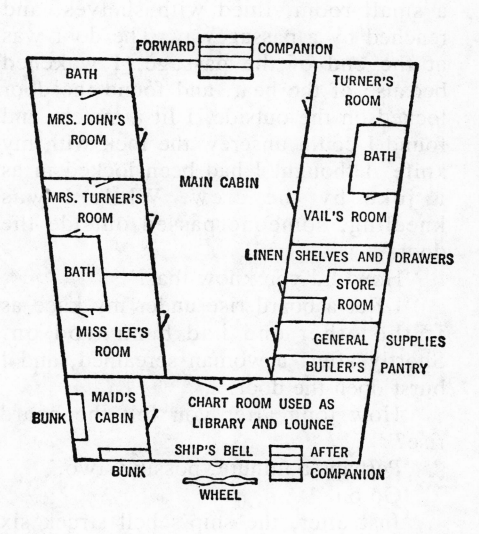

"State what happened on the night of August 12 and early morning of August 13."

"I slept in the storeroom in the after house. As it was very hot, I always left the door open. The storeroom itself was a small room, lined with shelves, and reached by a passageway. The door was at the end of the passage. I wakened because of the heat, and found the door locked on the outside. I lit a match, and found I could unscrew the lock with my knife. I thought I had been locked in as a joke by the crew. While I was kneeling, someone passed outside the door."

"How did you know that?"

"I flet a board rise under my knee as if the other end had been trod on. Shortly after, a woman screamed, and I burst open the door."

"How long after you felt the board rise?"

"Perhaps a minute, possibly two."

"Go on."

"Just after, the ship's bell struck six — three o'clock. The main cabin was dark. There was a light in the chartroom, from the binnacle light. I felt my way to Mr. Vail's room. I heard him breathing. His door was open. I struck a match and looked at him. He had stopped breathing.''

''What was the state of his bunk?''

''Disordered — horrible. He was almost hacked to pieces.''

''Go on.''

''I ran back and got my revolver. I thought there had been a mutiny —''

''Confine yourself to what you saw and did. The court is not interested in what you thought.''

''I am only trying to explain what I did. I ran back to the storeroom and got my revolver, and ran back through the chart-room to the after companion, which had a hood. I thought that if anyone was lying in ambush, the hood would protect me until I could get to the deck. I told the helmsman what had happened, and ran forward. Mr. Singleton was on the forecastle-head. We went below together, and found the captain lying at the foot of the forward companion, also dead,''

''At this time, had you called the owner of the ship?''

''No. I called him then. But I could not rouse him.''

''Explain what you mean by that.''

''He had been drinking.''

There followed a furious wrangle over this point; but the prosecuting attorney succeeded in having question and answer stand.

''What did you do next?''

''The mate had called the crew. I wakened Mrs. Turner, Miss Lee, and Mrs. Johns, and then went to the chart-room to call the women there. The door was open an inch or so. I received no answer to my knock, and pulled it open. Karen Hansen, the maid, was dead on the floor, and the stewardess was in her bunk, in a state of collapse.''

''State where you found the ax with which the crimes were committed.''

''It was found in the stewardess's bunk.''

''Where is this ax now?''

''It was stolen from the captain's

cabin, where it was locked for safe keeping, and presumably thrown overboard. At least, we did not find it.

"I see you are consulting a book to refresh your memory. What is this book?"

"The ship's log."

"How does it happen to be in your possession?"

"The crew appointed me captain. As such, I kept the log-book. It contains a full account of the discovery of the bodies, witnessed by all the men."

"Is it in your writing?"

"Yes; it is my writing."

"You read it to the men, and they signed it?"

"No; they read it themselves before they signed it."

After a wrangle as to my having authority to make a record in the log-book, the presecuting attorney succeeded in having the book admitted as evidence, and read to the jury the entry of August 13.

Having thus proved the crimes, I was excused, to be recalled later. The defense reserving its cross-examination, the doctor from the quarantine station was called next, and testified to the manner of death. His testimony was revolting, and bears in no way on the story, save in one particular — a curious uniformity in the mutilation of the bodies of Vail and Captain Richardson — a sinister similarity that was infinitely shocking. In each case the forehead, the two arms, and the abdomen had received a frightful blow. In the case of the Danish girl there was only one wound — the injury on the head.

Chapter 20

Oleson's Story

Henrietta Sloane was called next.

"Your name?"

"Henrietta Sloane."

"Are you married?"

"A widow."

"When and where were you born?"

"Isle of Man, December 11, 1872."

"How long have you lived in the United States?"

"Since I was two."

"Your position on the yacht *Ella?*"

"Stewardess."

"Before that?"

"On the *Baltic,* between Liverpool and New York. That was how I met Mrs. Turner."

"Where was your room on the yacht *Ella?*"

"Off the chart-room."

"Will you indicate on this diagram?"

"It was there." (Pointing.)

The diagram was shown to the jury.

"There are two bunks in this room. Which was yours?"

"The one at the side — the one opposite the door was Karen's."

"Tell what happened on the night of August 12 and the morning of the 13th."

"I went to bed early. Karen Hansen had not come down by midnight. When I opened the door, I saw why. Mr. Turner and Mr. Singleton were there drinking."

The defense objected to this but was overruled by the court.

"Mr. Vail was trying to persuade the mate to go on deck, before the captain came down."

"Did they go?"

"No."

"What comment did Mr. Singleton make?"

"He said he hoped the captain would come. He wanted a chance to get at him."

"What happened after that?"

"The captain came down and ordered the mate on deck. Mr. Vail and the captain got Mr. Turner to his room."

"How do you know that?"

"I opened my door."

"What then?"

"Karen came down at 12:30. We went to bed. At ten minutes to three the bell rang for Karen. She got up and put on a wrapper and slippers. She was grumbling and I told her to put out the light and let me sleep. As she opened the door she screamed and fell back on the floor. Something struck me on the shoulder, and I fainted. I learned later it was the ax."

"Did you hear any sound outside, before you opened the door?"

"A curious chopping sound. I spoke of it to her. It came from the chart-room."

"When the girl fell back into the room, did you see anyone beyond her?"

"I saw something — I couldn't say just what."

"Was what you saw a figure?"

"I — I am not certain. It was light

— almost white.''

''Can you not describe it?''

''I am afraid not — except that it seemed white.''

''How tall was it?''

''I couldn't say.''

''As tall as the girl?''

''Just about, perhaps.''

''Think of something that it resembled. This is important, Mrs. Sloane. You must make an effort.''

''I think it looked most like a fountain.''

Even the jury laughed at this, and yet, Mrs. Sloane was right — or nearly so!

''That is curious. How did it resemble a fountain?''

''Perhaps I should have said a fountain in moonlight — white, and misty, and — and flowing.''

''And yet, this curiously shaped object threw the ax at you, didn't it?''

There was no objection to the form of this question, but the court overruled it.

''I did not say *it* threw the ax. I did not see it thrown. I felt it.''

''Did you know the first mate,

Singleton, before you met on the *Ella?*"

"Yes, sir."

"Where?"

"We were on the same vessel two years ago, the *American*, for Bermuda."

"Were you friends?"

"Yes."

"Why did you break it off?"

"We differed about a good many things."

After a long battle, the prosecuting attorney was allowed to show that, following the breaking off of her relations with Singleton, she had been a witness against him in an assault-and-battery case, and had testified to his violence of temper. The dispute took so long that there was only time for her cross-examination. The effect of the evidence, so far, was distinctly bad for Singleton.

His attorney, Goldstein, cross-examined Mrs. Sloane.

Attorney for the defense: "Did you ever write a letter to the defendant, Mrs. Sloane, threatening him if he did not marry you?"

"I do not recall such a letter."

"Is this letter in your writing?"

"I think so. Yes."

"Mrs. Sloane, you testify that you 'opened your door and saw' Mr. Vail and the captain taking Mr. Turner to his room. Is this correct?"

"Yes."

"Why did they take him? I mean, was he not able, apparently, to walk alone?"

"He was able to walk. They walked beside him."

"In your testimony, taken at the time and entered in the ship's log, you say you 'judged by the sounds.' Here you say you 'opened the door and saw them.' Which is correct?"

"I saw them."

"You say that Mr. Singleton said he wished to 'get at' the captain. Are those his exact words?"

"I do not recall his exact words."

"Perhaps I can refresh your mind. With the permission of the court, I shall read from the ship's log this woman's statement, recorded by the man who was in charge of the vessel, and therefore competent to make such record, and signed by the witness as having been read and approved by her: —

" 'Mr. Singleton said that he hoped the captain would come, as he *and Mr. Turner* only wanted a chance to get at him. . . . There was a sound outside, and Karen thought it was Mr. Turner falling over something, and said that she hoped she would not meet him. Once or twice, when he had been drinking, he had made overtures to her, and she detested him. . . . She opened the door and came back in the room, touching me on the arm. ''That beast is out there,'' she said, ''sitting on the companion steps. If he tries to stop me, I'll call you.'' ' "

The reading made a profound impression. The prosecution, having succeeded in having the log admitted as evidence, had put a trump card in the hands of the defense.

"What were the relations between Mr. Turner and the captain?"

"I don't know what you mean."

"Were they friendly?"

"No — not very."

"Did you overhear, on the night of August 9, a conversation between Mr. Turner and Mr. Vail?"

"Yes."

"What was its nature?"

"They were quarreling."

"What did Williams, the butler, give you to hide, that night?"

"Mr. Turner's revolver."

"What did he say when he gave it to you?"

"He said to throw it overboard or there would be trouble."

"Mrs. Sloane, do you recognize these two garments?"

He held up a man's dinner shirt and a white waistcoat. The stewardess, who had been calm enough, started and paled.

"I cannot tell without examining them." (They were given to her, and she looked at them) "Yes, I have seen them."

"What are they?"

"A shirt and waistcoat of Mr. Turner's."

"When did you see them last?"

"I packed them in my trunk when we left the boat. They had been forgotten when the other trunks were packed."

"Had you washed them?"

"No."

"Were they washed on shipboard?"

"They look like it. They have not been ironed."

"Who gave them to you to pack in your trunk?"

"Mrs. Johns."

"What did you do with them on reaching New York?"

I left them in my trunk."

"Why did you not return them to Mr. Turner?"

"I was ill, and forgot. I'd like to know what right you have going through a person's things — and taking what you want!"

The stewardess was excused, the defense having scored perceptibly. It was clear what line the young lawyer intended to follow.

Oleson, the Swede, was called next, and after the usual formalities:—

"Where were you between midnight and 4 a.m. on the morning of August 13?"

"In the crow's nest of the *Ella*."

"State what you saw between midnight and one o'clock."

"I saw Mate Singleton walking on the forecastle-head. Every now and then he went to the rail. He seemed to be vomiting. It was too dark to see much. Then he went aft along the port side of the house, and came forward again on the starboard side. He went to where the ax was kept."

"Where was that?"

"Near the starboard corner of the forward house. All the Turner boats have an emergency box, with an ax and other tools, in easy reach. The officer on watch carried the key."

"Could you see what he was doing?"

"No; but he was fumbling at the box. I heard him."

"Where did he go after that?"

"He went aft."

"You could not see him?"

"I didn't look. I thought I saw

something white moving below me, and I was watching it.''

''This white thing — what did it look like?''

''Like a dog, I should say. It moved about, and then disappeared.''

''How?''

''I don't understand.''

''Over the rail?''

''Oh — no, sir. It faded away.''

''Had you ever heard talk among the men of the *Ella* being a haunted ship?''

''Yes — but not until after I'd signed on her!''

''Was there some talk of this 'white thing'?''

''Yes.''

''Before the murders?''

''No, sir; not till after. I guess I saw it first.''

''What did the men say about it?''

''They thought it scared Mr. Schwartz overboard. The *Ella's* been unlucky as to crews. They call her a 'devil ship.' ''

''Did you see Mr. Singleton on deck between two and three o'clock?''

''No, sir.''

The cross-examination was very short:—

"What sort of night was it?"

"Very dark."

"Would the first mate, as officer on watch, be supposed to see that the emergency case you speak of was in order?"

"Yes, sir."

"Did the officer on watch remain on the forecastle-head?"

"Mr. Schwartz did not; Mr. Singleton did, mostly except when he went back to strike the bells."

"Could Mr. Singleton have been on deck without you seeing him?"

"Yes, if he did not move around or smoke. I could see his pipe lighted."

"Did you see his pipe that night?"

"No, sir."

"If you were sick, would you be likely to smoke?"

This question, I believe, was ruled out.

"In case the wheel of the vessel were lashed for a short time, what would happen?"

"Depends on the weather. She'd be likely to come to or fall off considerable."

"Would the lookout know it?"

"Yes, sir."

"How?"

"The sails would show it, sir."

That closed the proceedings for the day. The crowd seemed reluctant to disperse. Turner's lawyers were in troubled consultation with him. Singleton was markedly more cheerful, and I thought the prosecution looked perturbed and uneasy. I went back to jail that night, and dreamed of Elsa — not as I had seen her that day, bending forward, watching every point of the evidence, but as I had seen her so often on the yacht, facing into the salt breeze as if she loved it, her hands in the pockets of her short white jacket, her hair blowing back from her forehead in damp, close-curling rings.

Chapter 21

"A Bad Woman"

Charlie Jones was called first, on the second day of the trial. He gave his place of birth as Pennsylvania, and his present shore address as a Sailors' Christian Home in New York. He offered, without solicitation, the information that he had been twenty-eight years in the Turner service, and could have been "up at the top," but preferred the forecastle, so that he could be an influence to the men.

His rolling gait, twinkling blue eyes, and huge mustache, as well as the plug of tobacco which he sliced with a huge knife, put the crowd in good humor, and relieved somewhat the somberness of the proceedings.

''Where were you between midnight

and 4 a.m. on the morning of August 13?''

''At the wheel.''

''You did not leave the wheel during that time?''

''Yes, sir.''

''When was that?''

''After they found the captain's body. I went to the forward companion and looked down.''

''Is a helmsman permitted to leave his post?''

''With the captain lying dead down in a pool of blood, I should think —''

''Never mind thinking. Is he?''

''No.''

''What did you do with the wheel when you left it?''

''Lashed it. There are two rope-ends, with loops, to lash it with. When I was on the *Sarah Winters* —''

''Stick to the question. Did you see the mate, Mr. Singleton, during your watch?''

''Every half-hour from 12:30 to 1:30. He struck the bells. After that he said he was sick. He thought he'd been poisoned. He said he was going forward to lie down, and for me to strike them.''

''Who struck the bell at three o'clock?''

''I did, sir.''

''When did you hear a woman scream?''

''Just before that.''

''What did you do?''

''Nothing. It was the Hansen woman. I didn't like her. She was a bad woman. When I told her what she was, she laughed.''

''Were you ever below in the after house?''

''No, sir; not since the boat was fixed up.''

''What could you see through the window beside the wheel?''

''It looked into the chart-room. If the light was on, I could see all but the floor.''

''Between the hours of 1 a.m. and 3 a.m., did anyone leave or enter the after house by the after companion?''

''Yes, sir. Mr. Singleton went down into the chart-room, and came back again in five or ten minutes."

"At what time?"

"At four bells — two o'clock."

"No one else?"

"No, sir; but I saw Mr. Turner —"

"Confine yourself to the question. What was Mr. Singleton's manner at the time you mention?"

"He was excited. He brought up a bottle of whisky from the chart-room table, and drank what was left in it. Then he muttered something, and threw the empty bottle over the rail. He said he was still sick."

The cross-examination confined itself to one detail of Charlie Jones's testimony.

"Did you, between midnight and 3 a.m., see anyone in the chart-room besides the mate?"

"Yes — Mr. Turner."

"You say you cannot see into the chart-room from the wheel at night. How did you see him?"

"He turned on the light. He seemed to be looking for something."

"Was he dressed?"

"Yes, sir."

"Can you describe what he wore?"

"Yes, sir. His coat was off. He had a white shirt and a white vest."

"Were the shirt and vest similar to these I show you?"

"Most of them things look alike to me. Yes, sir."

The defense had scored again. But it suffered at the hands of Burns, the next witness. I believe the prosecution had intended to call Turner at this time; but, after a whispered conference with Turner's attorneys, they made a change. Turner, indeed, was in no condition to go on the stand. He was pallid and twitching, and his face was covered with sweat.

Burns corroborated the testimony against Singleton — his surly temper, his outbursts of rage, his threats against the captain. And he brought out a new point: that Jones, the helmsman, had been afraid of Singleton that night, and had asked not to be left alone at the wheel.

During this examination the

prosecution for the first time made clear their position: that the captain was murdered first; that Vail interfered, and, pursued by Singleton, took refuge in his bunk, where he was slaughtered; that the murderer, bending to inspect his horrid work, had unwittingly touched the bell that roused Karen Hansen, and, crouching in the chart-room with the ax, had struck her as she opened the door.

The prosecution questioned Burns about the ax and its disappearance.

"Who suggested that the ax be kept in the captain's cabin?"

"Leslie, acting as captain."

"Who had the key?"

"I carried it on a strong line around my neck."

"Whose arrangement was that?"

"Leslie's. He had the key to Mr. Singleton's cabin, and I carried this one. We divided the responsibility."

"Did you ever give the key to anyone?"

"No, sir."

"Did it ever leave you?"

"Not until it was taken away."

"When was that?"

"On Saturday morning, August 23, shortly before dawn."

"Tell what happened."

"I was knocked down from behind, while I was standing at the port forward corner of the after house. The key was taken from me while I was unconscious."

"Did you ever see the white object that has been spoken of by the crew?"

"No, sir. I searched the deck one night when Adams, the lookout, raised an alarm. We found nothing except —"

"Go on."

"He threw down a marlinespike at something moving in the bow. The spike disappeared. We couldn't find it, although we could see where it had struck the deck. Afterward we found a marlinespike hanging over the ship's side by a lanyard. It might have been the one we looked for."

"Explain 'lanyard.' "

"A cord — a sort of rope."

"It could not have fallen over the side and hung there?"

"It was fastened with a Blackwell hitch."

"Show us what you mean."

On cross-examination by Singleton's attorney, Burns was forced to relate the incident of the night before his injury — that Mrs. Johns had asked to see the ax, and he had shown it to her. He maintained stoutly that she had not been near the bunk, and that the ax was there when he locked the door.

Adams, called, testified to seeing a curious, misty-white object on the forecastle-head. It had seemed to come over the bow. The marlinespike he threw had had no lanyard.

Mrs. Turner and Miss Lee escape with a light examination. Their evidence amounted to little, and was practically the same. They had retired early, and did not rouse until I called them. They remained in their rooms most of the time after that, and were busy caring for Mr. Turner, who had been ill. Mrs. Turner was good enough to say that I had made them as safe and as comfortable as possible.

The number of witnesses to be examained, and the searching grilling to which most of them were subjected, would have dragged the case to interminable length, had it not been for the attitude of the judges, who discouraged quibbling and showed a desire to reach the truth with the least possible delay. One of the judges showed the wide and unbiased attitude of the court by a little speech after an especially venomous contest.

"Gentlemen," he said, "we are attempting to get to a solution of this thing. We are trying one man, it is true, but, in a certain sense, we are trying every member of the crew, every person who was on board the ship the night of the crime. We have a curious situation. The murderer is before us, either in the prisoner's dock or among the witnesses. Let us get at the truth without bickering."

Mrs. Johns was called, following Miss Lee. I watched her carefully on the stand. I had never fathomed Mrs. Johns, or her attitude toward the rest of the party. I had thought, at the beginning of the cruise, that Vail and she were incipient lovers. But she had taken his death with a calmness that was close to indifference. There was something strange and inexplicable in her tigerish championship of Turner — and it remains inexplicable even now. I have wondered since — was she in love with Turner, or was she only a fiery partisan? I wonder!

She testified with an insolent coolness that clearly irritated the prosecution — thinking over her replies, refusing to recall certain things, and eyeing the jury with long, slanting glances that set them, according to their type, either wriggling or ogling.

The first questions were the usual ones. Then: —

"Do you recall the night of the 31st of July?"

"Can you be more specific?"

"I refer to the night when Captain Richardson found the prisoner in the chart-room and ordered him on deck."

"I recall that, yes."

"Where were you during the quarrel?"

"I was behind Mr. Vail."

"Tell us about it, please."

"It was an ordinary brawl. The captain knocked the mate down."

"Did you hear the mate threaten the captain?"

"No. He went on deck, muttering; I did not hear what he said."

"After the crimes, what did you do?"

"We established a deadline at the foot of the forward companion. The other was locked."

"Was there a guard at the top of the companion?"

"Yes; but we trusted no one."

"Where was Mr. Turner?"

"Ill, in his cabin."

"How ill?"

"Very. He was delirious."

"Did you allow anyone down?"

"At first, Leslie, a sort of cabin-boy and deck-steward, who seemed to know something of medicine. Afterward we would not allow him, either."

"Why?"

"We did not trust him."

"This Leslie — why had you asked him to sleep in the storeroom?"

"I — was afraid."

"Will you explain why you were afraid?"

"Fear is difficult to explain, isn't it? If one knows why one is afraid, one — er — generally isn't."

"That's a bit subtle, I'm afraid. You were afraid, then, without knowing why?"

"Yes."

"Had you a revolver on board?"

"Yes."

"Whose revolver was kept on the cabin table?"

"Mine. I always carry one."

"Always?"

"Yes."

"Then — have you one with you now?"

"Yes."

"When you asked the sailor Burns to let you see the ax, what did you give as a reason?'

"The truth — curiosity."

"Then, having seen the ax, where did you go?"

"Below."

"Please explain the incident of the two articles Mr. Goldstein showed to the jury yesterday, the shirt and waistcoat."

"That was very simple. Mr. Turner had been very ill. We took turns in caring for him. I spilled a bowl of broth over the garments that were shown, and rubbed them out in the bathroom. They were hung in the cabin used by Mr. Vail to dry, and I forgot them when we were packing."

The attorney for the defense cross-examined her: —

"What color were the stains you speak of?"

"Darkish — red-brown."

"What sort of broth did you spill?"

"That's childish, isn't it? I don't recall."

"You recall its color."

"It was beef broth."

"Mrs. Johns, on the night you visited the forward house and viewed the ax, did you visit it again?"

"The ax, or the forward house?"

"The house."

She made one of her long pauses. Finally: —

"Yes."

"When?"

"Between three and four o'clock."

"Who went with you?"

"I went alone."

"Why did you go beyond the line that was railed off for your safety?"

(Sharply.) "Because I wished to. I was able to take care of myself."

"Why did you visit the forward house?"

"I was nervous and could not sleep. I thought no one safe while the ax was on the ship."

"Did you see the body of Burns, the sailor, lying on the deck at that time?"

"He might have been there; I did not see him."

"Are you saying that you went to the forward house to throw the ax overboard?"

"Yes — if I could get in."

"Did you know why the ax was

being kept?''

''Because the murders had been committed with it.''

''Had you heard of any finger-prints on the handle?''

''No.''

''Did it occur to you that you were interfering with justice in disposing of the ax?''

''Do you mean justice or law? They are not the same.''

''Tell us about your visit to the forward house.''

''It was between two and three. I met no one. I had a bunch of keys from the trunks and from four doors in the after house. Miss Lee knew I intended to try to get rid of the ax. I did not need my keys. The door was open — wide open. I — I went in, and —''

Here, for the first time, Mrs. Johns's composure forsook her. She turned white, and her maid passed up to her a silver smelling-salts bottle.

''What happened when you went in?''

''It was dark. I stood just inside. Then — something rushed past me and out of the door, a something — I don't know what — a woman, I thought at first, in white.''

''If the room was dark, how could you tell it was white?''

''There was a faint light — enough to see that. There was no noise — just a sort of swishing sound.''

''What did you do then?''

''I waited a moment, and hurried back to the after house.''

''Was the ax gone then?''

''I do not know.''

''Did you see the ax at that time?''

''No.''

''Did you touch it?''

''I have never touched it, at that time or before.''

She could not be shaken in her testimony and was excused. She had borne her grilling exceedingly well, and, in spite of her flippancy, there was a ring of sincerity about the testimony that gave it weight.

Following her evidence, the testimony of Tom, the cook, made things look bad for Singleton, by connecting him with

Mrs. Johns's intruder in the captain's room. He told of Singleton's offer to make him a key to the galley with wire. It was clear that Singleton had been a prisoner in name only, and this damaging statement was given weight when, on my recall later, I identified the bunch of keys, the file, and the club that I had taken from Singleton's mattress. It was plain enough that, the attack on Burns and the disappearnce of the ax were easily enough accounted for. It would have been possible, also, to account for the white figure that had so alarmed the men, on the same hypothesis.

Cross-examination of Tom by Mr. Goldstein, Singleton's attorney, brought out one curious fact. He had made no dark soup or broth for the after house. Turner had taken nothing during his illness but clam bouillon, made with milk, and the meals served to the four women had been very light. "They lived on toast and tea, mostly," he said.

That completed the taking of evidence for the day. In spite of the struggles of the clever young lawyer, the weight of testimony was against Singleton. But there were curious discrepancies.

Turner went on the stand the next morning.

Chapter 22

Turner's Story

"Your name?"

"Marshall Benedict Turner."

"Your residence?"

"— West 106th Street, New York City."

"Your occupation?"

"Member of the firm of L. Turner's Sons, shipowners. In the coast trade."

"Do you own the yacht *Ella?*"

"Yes."

"Do you recognize this chart?"

"Yes. It is the chart of the after house of the *Ella*."

"Will you show where your room is on the drawing?"

"Here."

"And Mr. Vail's?"

"Next, connecting through a bathroom."

"Where was Mr. Vail's bed on that chart?"

"Here against the storeroom wall."

"With your knowledge of the ship and its partitions, do you think that a crime could be committed, a crime of the violent nature of this one, without making a great deal of noise and being heard in the storeroom?"

Violent opposition developing to this question, it was changed in form and broken up. Eventually, Turner answered that the partitions were heavy and he thought it possible.

"Were the connecting doors between your room and Mr. Vail's generally locked at night?"

"Yes. Not always."

"Were they locked on this particular night?"

"I don't remember."

"When did you see Mr. Vail last?"

"At midnight, or about that. I — I was not well. He went with me to my room."

"What were your relations with Mr. Vail?"

"We were old friends."

"Did you hear any sound in Mr. Vail's cabin that night?"

"None. But, as I say, I was — ill. I might not have noticed."

"Did you leave your cabin that night of August 12 or early morning of the 13th?"

"Not that I remember."

"The steersman has testified to seeing you, without your coat, in the chart-room, at two o'clock. Were you there?"

"I may have been — I think not."

"Why do you say you 'may have been — I think not'?"

"I was ill. The next day I was delirious. I remember almost nothing of that time."

"Did you know the woman Karen Hansen?"

"Only as a maid in my wife's employ."

"Did you hear the crash when Leslie broke down the door of the storeroom?"

"No. I was in a sort of stupor."

"Did you know the prisoner before you employed him on the *Ella?*"

"Yes; he had been in our employ several times."

"What was his reputation — I mean, as a ship's officer?"

"Good."

"Do you recall the night of the 31st of July?"

"Quite well."

"Please tell what you know about it."

"I had asked Mr. Singleton below to have a drink with me. Captain Richardson came below and ordered him on deck. They had words, and he knocked Singleton down."

"Did you hear the mate threaten to 'get' the captain, then or later?"

"He may have made some such threat."

"Is there a bell in your cabin connecting with the maids' cabin off the chart-room?"

"No. My bell rang in the room back of the galley, where Williams slept. The boat was small, and I left my man at home. Williams looked after me."

"Where did the bell from Mr. Vail's room ring?"

"In the maids' room. Mr. Vail's room was designed for Mrs. Turner. When we asked Mrs. Johns to go with us, Mrs. Turner gave Vail her room. It was a question of baths."

"Did you ring any bell during the night?"

"No."

"Knowing the relation of the bell above Mr. Vail's berth to the bed itself, do you think he could have reached it after his injury?"

(Slowly.) "After what the doctor has said, no; he would have had to raise himself and reach up."

The cross-examination was brief but to the point: —

"What do you mean by 'ill'?"

"That night I had been somewhat ill; the next day I was in bad shape."

"Did you know the woman Karen Hansen before your wife employed her?"

"No."

"A previous witness has said that the Hansen woman, starting out of her room, saw you outside and retreated.

Were you outside the door at any time during that night?''

''Only before midnight.''

''You said you 'might have been' in the chart-room at two o'clock.''

''I have said I was ill. I *might* have done almost anything.''

''That is exactly what we are getting at, Mr. Turner. Going back to the 31st of July, when you were *not* ill, did you have any words with the captain?''

''We had a few. He was exceeding his authority.''

''Do you recall what you said?''

''I was indignant.''

''Think again, Mr. Turner. If you cannot recall, someone else will.''

''I threatened to dismiss him and put the first mate in his place. I was angry, naturally.''

''And what did the captain reply?''

''He made me an absurd threat to put me in irons.''

''What were your relations after that?''

''They were strained. We simply avoided each other.''

"Just a few more questions, Mr. Turner, and I shall not detain you. Do you carry a key to the emergency case in the forward house, the case that contained the ax?"

Like many of the questions, this was disputed hotly. It was finally allowed, and Turner admitted the key. Similar cases were carried on all the Turner boats, and he had such a key on his ring.

"Did you ever see the white object that terrified the crew?"

"Never. Sailors are particularly liable to such — hysteria."

"During your delirium, did you ever see such a figure?"

"I do not recall any details of that part of my illness."

"Were you in favor of bringing the bodies back to port?"

"I — yes, certainly."

"Do you recall going on deck the morning after the murders were discovered?"

"Vaguely."

"What were the men doing at

that time?''

''I believe — really, I do not like to repeat so often that I was ill that day.''

''Have you any recollection of what you said to the men at that time?''

''None.''

''Let me refresh your memory from the ship's log: —

(Reading.) '' 'Mr. Turner insisted that the bodies be buried at sea, and, on the crew opposing this, retired to his cabin, announcing that he considered the attitude of the men a mutiny.' ''

''I recall being angry at the men — not much else. My position was rational enough, however. It was midsummer, and we had a long voyage before us.''

''I wish to read something else to you. The witness Leslie testified to sleeping in the storeroom, at the request of Mrs. Johns'' (reading), '' 'giving as her reason a fear of something going wrong, as there was trouble between Mr. Turner and the captain.' ''

Whatever question Mr. Goldstein had been framing, he was not permitted to use this part of the record. The log was admissible only as a record on the spot, made by a competent person and witnessed by all concerned, of the actual occurrences on the *Ella*. My record of Mrs. Johns's remark was ruled out; Turner was not on trial.

Turner, pale and shaking, left the stand at two o'clock that day, and I was recalled. My earlier testimony had merely established the finding of the bodies. I was now to have a bad two hours. I was an important witness, probably the most important. I had heard the scream that had revealed the tragedy, and had been in the main cabin of the after house only a moment or so after the murderer. I found the bodies, Vail still living, and had been with the accused mate when he saw the captain prostrate at the foot of the forward companion.

All of this, aided by skillful questions, I told as exactly as possible. I told of the mate's strange manner on finding the bodies; I related, to a breathless quiet, the placing of the bodies in the jolly-boat, and the reading of the burial service over them; I told of the little boat that followed us, like some avenging spirit, carrying by day a small American flag, union down, and at night a white light. I told of having to increase the length of the towing-line as the heat grew greater, and of a fear I had that the rope would separate, or that the mysterious hand that was the author of the misfortunes would cut the line.

I told of the long nights without sleep, while, with our few available men, we tried to work the *Ella* back to land; of guarding the after house; of a hundred false alarms that set our nerves quivering and our hearts leaping. And I made them feel, I think, the horror of a situation where each man suspected his neighbor, feared and loathed him, and yet stayed close by him because a known danger is better than an unknown horror.

The record of my examination is particularly faulty, McWhirter having allowed personal feeling to interfere with accuracy. Here and there in the margins of his notebook I find unflattering allusions to the prosecuting attorney; and after one question, an impeachment of my motives, to which Mac took violent exception, no answer at all is recorded, and in a furious scrawl is written: "The —— little whippersnapper! Leslie could smash him between his thumb and finger!"

I found another curious record — a leaf, torn out of the book, and evidently designed to be sent to me, but failing its destination, was as follows: "For Heaven's sake, don't look at the girl so much! The newspaper men are on."

But, to resume my examination. The first questions were not of particular interest. Then: —

"Did the prisoner know you had moved to the after house?"

"I do not know. The forecastle hands knew."

"Tell what you know of the quarrel on July 31st between Captain Richardson and the prisoner."

"I saw it from a deck window." I described it in detail.

"Why did you move to the after house?"

"At the request of Mrs. Johns. She said she was nervous."

"What reason did she give?"

"That Mr. Turner was in a dangerous mood; he had quarreled with the captain and was quarreling with Mr. Vail."

"Did you know the arrangement of rooms in the after house? How the people slept?"

"In a general way."

"What do you mean by that?"

"I knew Mr. Vail's room and Miss Lee's."

"Did you know where the maids slept?"

"Yes."

"You have testified that you were locked in. Was the key kept in the lock?"

"Yes."

"Would whoever locked you in have had only to move the key from one side of the door to the other?"

"Yes"

"Was the key left in the lock when

you were fastened in?''

''No.''

''Now, Dr. Leslie, we want you to tell us what the prisoner did that night when you told him what had happened.''

''I called to him to come below, for God's sake. He seemed dazed and at a loss to know what to do. I told him to get his revolver and call the captain. He went into the forward house and got his revolver, but he did not call the captain. We went below and stumbled over the captain's body.''

''What was the mate's condition?''

''When we found the body?''

''His general conditon.''

''He was intoxicated. He collapsed on the steps when we found the captain. We both almost collapsed.''

''What was his mental condition?''

''If you mean, was he frightened, we both were.''

''Was he pale?''

''I did not notice then. He was pale and looked ill later, when the crew gathered.''

''About this key: was it ever found?

The key to the storeroom?''

''Yes.''

''When?''

''That same morning.''

''Where? And by whom?''

''Miss Lee found it on the floor in Mr. Turner's room.''

The prosecution was totally unprepared for this reply, and proceedings were delayed for a moment while the attorneys consulted. On the resumption of my examination, they made a desperate attempt to impeach my character as a witness, trying to show that I had sailed under false pretenses; that I was so feared in the after house that the women refused to allow me below, or to administer to Mr. Turner the remedies I prepared; and, finally, that I had surrendered myself to the crew as a suspect, of my own accord.

Against this the cross-examination threw all its weight. The prosecuting attorneys having dropped the question of the key, the shrewd young lawyer for the defense followed it up: —

''This key, Dr. Leslie, do you know

where it is now?''

''Yes; I have it.''

''Will you tell how it came into your possession?''

''Certainly. I picked it up on the deck, a night or so after the murders. Miss Lee had — dropped it.'' I caught Elsa Lee's eye, and she gave me a warm glance of gratitude.

''Have you the key with you?''

''Yes.'' I produced it.

''Are you a football player, Doctor?''

''I was.''

''I thought I recalled you. I have seen you play several times. In spite of our friend the attorney for the commonwealth, I do not believe we will need to call character witnesses for you. Did you see Miss Lee pick up the key to the storeroom in Mr. Turner's room?''

''Yes.''

''Did it occur to you at the time that the key had any significance?''

''I wondered how it got there.''

''You say you listened inside the locked door, and heard no sound, but felt a board rise up under your knee. A moment or two later, when you called the prisoner, he was intoxicated, and reeled. Do you mean to tell us that a drunken man could have made his way in the darkness, through a cabin filled with chairs, tables, and a piano, in absolute silence?''

The prosecuting attorney was on his feet in an instant, and the objection was sustained. I was next shown the keys, club, and file taken from Singleton's mattress. ''You have identified these objects as having been found concealed in the prisoner's mattress. Do any of these keys fit the captain's cabin?''

''No.''

''Who saw the prisoner during the days he was locked in his cabin?''

''I saw him occasionally. The cook saw him when he carried him his meals.''

''Did you ever tell the prisoner where the ax was kept?''

''No.''

''Did the members of the crew know?''

''I believe so. Yes.''

"Was the fact that Burns carried the key to the captain's cabin a matter of general knowledge?"

"No. The crew knew that Burns and I carried the keys; they did not know which one each carried, unless — "

"Go on, please."

"If anyone had seen Burns take Mrs. Johns forward and show her the ax, he would have known."

"Who were on deck at that time?"

"All the crew were on deck, the forecastle being closed. In the crow's nest was McNamara; Jones was at the wheel."

"From the crow's nest could the lookout have seen Burns and Mrs. Johns going forward?"

"No. The two houses were connected by an awning."

"What could the helmsman see?"

"Nothing forward of the after house."

The prosecution closed its case with me. The defense, having virtually conducted its case by cross-examination of the witnesses already called, contented itself with producing a few character witnesses, and ''rested.'' Goldstein made an eloquent plea of ''no case,'' and asked the judge so to instruct the jury.

This was refused, and the case went to the jury on the seventh day — a surprisingly short trial, considering the magnitude of the crime.

The jury disagreed. But, while they wrangled, McWhirter and I were already on the right track. At the very hour that the jurymen were being discharged and steps taken for a retrial, we had the murderer locked in my room in a cheap lodging-house off Chestnut Street.

Chapter 23

Free Again

With the submission of the case to the jury, the witnesses were given their freedom. McWhirter had taken a room for me for a day or two to give me time to look about; and, his own leave of absence from his hospital being for ten days, we had some time together.

My situation was better than it had been in the summer. I had my strength again, although the long confinement had told on me. But my position was precarious enough. I had my pay from the *Ella,* and nothing else. And McWhirter, with a monthly stipend from his hospital of twenty-five dollars, was not much better off.

My first evening of freedom we spent at the theater. We bought the best seats in the house, and we dressed for the occasion — being in the position of having nothing to wear between shabby everyday wear and evening clothes.

"It is by way of celebration," Mac said, as he put a dab of shoe-blacking over a hole in his sock; "you having been restored to life, liberty, and the pursuit of happiness. That's the game, Leslie — the pursuit of happiness."

I was busy with a dress tie that I had washed and dried by pasting it on a mirror, an old trick of mine when funds ran low. I was trying to enter into Mac's festive humor, but I had not reacted yet from the horrors of the past few months.

"Happiness!" I said scornfully. "Do you call this happiness?"

He put up the blacking, and, coming to me, stood eyeing me in the mirror as I arranged my necktie.

"Don't be bitter," he said. "Happiness was my word. The Good Man was good to you when He made you. That ought to be a source of satisfaction. And as for the girl —"

"What girl?"

"If she could see you now. Why in thunder didn't you take those clothes on board? I wanted you to. Couldn't a captain wear a dress suit on special occasions?"

"Mac," I said gravely, "if you will think a moment, you will remember that the only special occasions on the *Ella*, after I took charge, were funerals. Have you sat through seven days of horrors without realizing that?"

Mac had once gone to Europe on a liner, and, having exhausted his funds, returned on a cattle-boat.

"All the captains I ever knew," he said largely, "were a fussy lot — dressed to kill, and navigating the boat from the head of a dinner-table. But I suppose you know. I was only regretting that she hadn't seen you the way you're looking now. That's all. I suppose I may regret, without hurting your feelings!"

He dropped all mention of Elsa after that, for a long time. But I saw him looking at me, at intervals, during the evening, and sighing. He was still regretting!

We enjoyed the theater, after all, with the pent-up enthusiasm of long months of work and strain. We laughed at the puerile fun, encored the prettiest of the girls, and swaggered in the lobby between acts, with cigarettes. There we ran across the one man I knew in Philadelphia, and had supper after the play with three or four fellows who, on hearing my story, persisted in believing that I had sailed on the *Ella* as a lark or to follow a girl. My simple statement that I had done it out of necessity met with roars of laughter and finally I let it go at that.

It was after one when we got back to the lodging-house, being escorted there in a racing car by a riotous crowd that stood outside the door, as I fumbled for my key, and screeched in unison: "Leslie! Leslie! Leslie! Sic 'em!" before they drove away.

The light in the dingy lodging-house parlor was burning full, but the hall was dark. I stopped inside and lighted a cigarette.

"Life, liberty, and the pursuit of

happiness, Mac!'' I said. ''I've got the first two, and the other can be had — for the pursuit.''

Mac did not reply: he was staring into the palor. Elsa Lee was standing by a table, looking at me.

She was very nervous, and tried to explain her presence in a breath — with the result that she broke down utterly and had to stop. Mac, his jovial face rather startled, was making for the stairs; but I sternly brought him back and presented him. Whereon, being utterly confounded, he made the tactful remark that he would have to go and put out the milk-bottles: it was almost morning!

She had been waiting since ten o'clock, she said. A taxicab, with her maid, was at the door. They were going back to New York in the morning, and things were terribly wrong.

''Wrong?'' You need not mind Mr. McWhirter. He is as anxious as I am to be helpful.''

''There are detectives watching Marshall; we saw one today at the hotel.

If the jury disagrees — and the lawyers think they will — they will arrest him.''

I thought it probable. There was nothing I could say. McWhirter made an effort to reassure her.

''It wouldn't be a hanging matter, anyhow,'' he said. ''There's a lot against him, but hardly a jury in the country would hang a man for something he did, if he could prove he was delirious the next day.'' She paled at this dubious comfort, but it struck her sense of humor, too, for she threw me a fleeting smile.

''I was to ask you to do something,'' she said. ''None of us can, for we are being watched. I was probably followed here. The *Ella* is still in the river, with only a watchman on board. We want you to go there tonight, if you can.''

''To the *Ella?*''

She was feeling in her pocketbook, and now she held out to me an envelope addressed in a sprawling hand to Mr. Turner at his hotel.

''Am I to open it?''

''Please.''

I unfolded the sheet of ruled note-paper of the most ordinary variety. It had been opened and laid flat, and on it, in black ink, was a crude drawing of the deck of the *Ella*, as one would look down on it from aloft. Here and there were small crosses in red ink, overlying it all from bow to stern, a red ax. Around the border, not written, but printed in childish letters, were the words: NOT YET. HA, HA. In a corner was a drawing of a gallows, or what passes in the everyday mind for a gallows, and in the opposite corner an open book.

"You see," she said, "it was mailed downtown late this afternoon. The hotel got it at seven o'clock. Marshall wanted to get a detective, but I thought of you. I knew — you knew the boat, and then — you had said —"

"Anything in all the world that I can do to help you, I will do," I said, looking at her. And the thing that I could not keep out of my eyes made her drop hers.

"Sweet little document!" said

McWhirter, looking over my shoulder. "Sent by someone with a nice disposition. What do the crosses mark?"

"The location of the bodies when found," I explained — "these three. This looks like the place where Burns lay unconscious. That one near the rail I don't know about, nor this by the mainmast."

"We thought they might mark places, clues, perhaps, that had been overlooked. The whole — the whole document is a taunt, isn't it? The scaffold, and the ax, and 'not yet'; a piece of bravado!"

"Right you are," said McWhirter admiringly. "A little escape of glee from somebody who's laughing too soon. One-thirty — it will soon be the proper hour for something to happen on the *Ella,* won't it? If that was sent by some member of the crew — and it looks like it; they are loose today — the quicker we follow it up, the better, if there's anything to follow."

"We thought if you would go early in the morning, before any of them make an excuse to go back on board —''

''We will go right away; but, please — don't build too much on this. It's a good possibility, that's all. Will the watchman let us on board?''

''We thought of that. Here is a note to him from Marshall, and — will you do us one more kindness?''

''I will.''

''Then — if you should find anything, bring it to us; to the police, later, if you must, but to us first.''

''When?''

''In the morning. We will not leave until we hear from you.''

She held out her hand, first to McWhirter, then to me. I kept it a little longer than I should have, perhaps, and she did not take it away.

''It is such a comfort,'' she said, ''to have you with us and not against us! For Marshall didn't do it, Leslie — I mean — it is hard for me to think of you as Dr. Leslie! He didn't do it. At first, we thought he might have, and he was delirious and could not reassure us. He swears he did not. I think, just at first, he was afraid he had done it; but he did not. I believe that, and you must.''

I believed her — I believed anything she said. I think that if she had chosen to say that I had wielded the murderer's ax on the *Ella,* I should have gone to the gallows rather than gainsay her. From that night, I was the devil's advocate, if you like. I was determined to save Marshall Turner.

She wished us to take her taxicab, dropping her at her hotel; and, reckless now of everything but being with her, I would have done so. But McWhirter's discreet cough reminded me of the street-car level of our finances, and I made the excuse of putting on more suitable clothing.

I stood in the street, bareheaded, watching her taxicab as it rattled down the street. McWhirter touched me on the arm.

''Wake up!'' he said. ''We have work to do, my friend.''

We went upstairs together, cautiously, not to rouse the house. At the top, Mac turned and patted me on the elbow, my shoulder being a foot or so above him.

''Good boy!'' he said. ''And if that shirt-front and tie didn't knock into eternal oblivion the deck-washing on the *Ella*, I'll eat them!''

Chapter 24

The Thing

I deserve no credit for the solution of the *Ella's* mystery. I have a certain quality of force, perhaps, and I am not lacking in physical courage; but I have no finesse of intellect. McWhirter, a foot shorter than I, round of face, jovial and stocky, has as much subtlety in his little finger as I have in my six feet and a fraction of body.

All the way to the river, therefore, he was poring over the drawing. He named the paper at once.

"Ought to know it," he said, in reply to my surprise. "Sold enough paper at the drugstore to qualify as a stationery engineer." He writhed as was his habit over his jokes, and then fell to work at the drawing again. "A book," he said, "and an ax, and a gibbet or gallows. B-

283

a-g — that make 'bag.' Doesn't go far, does it? Humorous duck, isn't he? Anyone who can write 'ha! ha!' under a gallows has a real humor. G-a-b, b-a-g!''

The *Ella* still lay in the Delaware, half a mile or so from her original moorings. She carried theusual riding lights — a white one in the bow, another at the stern, and the two vertical red lights which showed her not under command. In reply to repeated signals, we were unable to rouse the watchman. I had brought an electric flash with me, and by its aid we found a rope ladder over the side, with a small boat at its foot.

Although the boat indicated the presence of the watchman on board, we made our way to the deck without challenge. Here McWhirter suggested that the situation might be disagreeable, were the man to waken and get at us with a gun.

We stood by the top of the ladder, therefore, and made another effort to rouse him. "Hey, watchman!" I called. And McWhirter, in a deep bass, sang

lustily: "Watchman, what of the night?"
Neither of us made any perceptible
impression on the silence and gloom of
the *Ella*.

McWhirter grew less gay. The
deserted decks of the ship, her tragic
history, her isolation, the darkness,
which my small flash seemed only to
intensify, all had their effect on him.

"It's got my goat," he admitted. "It
smells like a tomb."

"Don't be an ass."

"Turn the light over the side and see
if we fastened that boat. We don't want
to be left here indefinitely."

"That's folly, Mac," I said, but I
obeyed him. "The watchman's boat is
there, so we —"

But he caught me suddenly by the arm
and shook me.

"My God!" he said. "What is that
over there?"

It was a moment before my eyes, after
the flashlight, could discern anything in
the darkness. Mac was pointing forward.
When I could see, Mac was ready to
laugh at himself.

"I told you the place had my goat!" he said sheepishly. "I thought I saw something duck around the corner of that building; but I think it was a ray from the searchlight on one of those boats."

"The watchman, probably," I said quietly. But my heart beat a little faster. "The watchman taking a look at us and gone for his gun."

I thought rapidly. If Mac had seen anything, I did not believe it was the watchman. But there should be a watchman on board — in the forward house, probably. I gave Mac my revolver and put the light in my pocket. I might want both hands that night. I saw better without the flash, and, guided partly by the bow light, partly by my knowledge of the yacht, I led the way across the deck. The forward house was closed and locked, and no knocking produced any indication of life. The after house we found not only locked, but barred across with strips of wood nailed into place. The forecastle was likewise closed. It was a dead ship.

No figure reappearing to alarm him,

Mac took the drawing out of his pocket and focused the flashlight on it.

"This cross by the mainmast," he said — "that would be where?"

"Right behind you, there."

He walked to the mast, and examined carefully around its base. There was nothing there, and even now I do not know to what that cross alluded, unless poor Schwartz —!

"Then this other one — forward, you call it, don't you? Suppose we locate that."

All expectation of the watchman having now died, we went forward on the port side to the approximate location of the cross. This being in the neighborhood where Mac had thought he saw something move, we approached with extreme caution. But nothing more ominous was discovered than the port lifeboat, nothing more ghostly heard than the occasional creak with which it rocked in its davits.

The lifeboat seemed to be indicated by the cross. It swung almost shoulder-high on McWhirter. We looked under and around it, with a growing feeling that we had misread the significance of the crosses, or that the sinister record extended to a time before the ''she devil'' of the Turner line was dressed in white and turned into a lady.

I was feeling underneath the boat, with a sense of absurdity that McWhirter put into words. ''I only hope,'' he said, ''that the watchman does not wake up now and see us. He'd be justified in filling us with lead, or putting us in strait-jackets.''

But I had discovered something.

''Mac,'' I said, ''someone has been at this boat within the last few minutes.''

''Why?''

''Take your revolver and watch the deck. One of the *barécas* —''

''What's that?''

''One of the water-barrels has been upset, and the plug is out. It is leaking into the boat. It is leaking fast, and there's only a gallon or so in the bottom! Give me the light.''

The contents of the boat revealed the truth of what I had said. The boat was in confusion. Its cover had been thrown back, and tins of biscuit, bailers, boat-hooks and extra rowlocks were jumbled together in confusion. The *barécas* lay on its side, and its plug had been either knocked or drawn out.

McWhirter was for turning to inspect the boat; but I ordered him sternly to watch the deck. He was inclined to laugh at my caution, which he claimed was a quality in me he had not suspected. He lounged against the rail near me, and, in spite of his chaff, kept a keen enough lookout.

The *barécas* of water were lashed amidships. In the bow and stern were small air-tight compartments, and in the stern was also a small locker from which the biscuit tins had been taken. I was about to abandon my search, when I saw something gleaming in the locker, and reached in and drew it out. It appeared to be an ordinary white sheet, but its presence there was curious. I turned the light on it. It was covered with dark-brown stains.

Even now the memory of that sheet

turns me ill. I shook it out, and Mac, at my exclamation, came to me. It was not a sheet at all, that is, not a whole one. It was a circular piece of white cloth, on which, in black, were curious marks — a six-pointed star predominating. There were others — a crescent, a crude attempt to draw what might be either a dog or a lamb, and a cross. From edge to edge it was smeared with blood.

Of what followed just after, both McWhirter and I are vague. There seemed to be, simultaneously, a yell of fury from the rigging overhead, and the crash of a falling body on the deck near us. Then we were closing with a kicking, biting, screaming thing, that bore me to the ground, extinguishing the little electric flash, and that, rising suddenly from under me, had McWhirter in the air, and almost overboard before I caught him. So dazed were we by the onslaught that the thing — whatever it was — could have escaped, and left us none the wiser. But, although it eluded us in the darkness, it did not leave. It was there, whimpering to itself, searching for something — the sheet. As I steadied Mac, it passed me. I caught at it. Immediately the struggle began all over again. But this time we had the advantage, and kept it. After a battle that seemed to last all night, and that was actually fought all over that part of the deck, we held the creature subdued, and Mac, getting a hand free, struck a match.

It was Charlie Jones.

That, after all, is the story. Jones was a madman, a homicidal maniac of the worst type. Always a madman, the homicidal element of his disease was recurrent and of a curious nature. He thought himself a priest of heaven, appointed to make ghastly sacrifices at certain signals from on high. The signals I am not sure of; he turned taciturn after his capture and would not talk. I am inclined to think that a shooting star, perhaps in a particular quarter of the heavens, was his signal. This is distinctly possible, and is made probable by the stars which he had painted with tar on his sacrificial robe.

The story of the early morning of August 13 will never be fully known; but much of it, in view of our knowledge, we were able to reconstruct. Thus — Jones ate his supper that night, a mild and well-disposed individual. During the afternoon before, he had read prayers for the soul of Schwartz, in whose departure he may or may not have had a part — I am inclined to think not, Jones construing his mission as being one to remove the wicked and the oppressor, and Schwartz hardly coming under either classification.

He was at the wheel from midnight until four in the morning on the night of the murders. At certain hours we believe that he went forward to the forecastle-head, and performed, clad in his priestly robe, such devotions as his disordered mind dictated. It is my idea that he looked, at these times, for a heavenly signal, either a meteor or some strange appearance of the heavens. It was known that he was a poor sleeper, and spent much time at night wandering around.

On the night of the crimes it is probable that he performed his devotions early, and then got the signal. This is evidenced by Singleton's finding the ax against the captain's door before midnight. He had evidently been disturbed. We believe that he intended to kill the captain and Mr. Turner, but made a mistake in the rooms. He clearly intended to kill the Danish girl. Several passages in his Bible, marked with a red cross, showed his inflamed hatred of loose women; and he believed Karen Hansen to be of that type.

He locked me in, slipping down from the wheel to do so, and pocketing the key. The night was fairly quiet. He could lash the wheel safely, and he had in his favor the fact that Oleson, the lookout, was a slow-thinking Swede who notoriously slept on his watch. He found the ax, not where he had left it, but back in the case. But the case was only closed, not locked — Singleton's error.

Armed with the ax, Jones slipped back to the wheel and waited. He had plenty of time. He had taken his robe from its hiding-place in the boat, and had it concealed near him with the ax. He was ready, but he was waiting for another signal. He got it at half-past two. He admitted the signal at the time, but concealed its nature — I think it was a shooting star. He killed Vail first, believing him to be Turner, and making with his ax the four signs of his cross. Then he went to the Hansen girl's door. He did not know about the bell, and probably rang it by accident as he leaned over to listen if Vail still breathed.

The captain, in the meantime, had been watching Singleton. He had forbidden his entering the after house; if he caught him disobeying he meant to put him in irons. He was without shoes or coat, and he sat waiting on the after companion steps for developments. It was the captain, probably whom Karen Hansen mistook for Turner. Later he went back to the forward companionway, either on his way back to his cabin, or still with an eye on Singleton's movements.

To the captain there must have appeared this grisly figure in flowing white, smeared with blood and armed with an ax. The sheet was worn over Jones's head — a long, narrow slit serving him to see through, and two other slits freeing his arms. The captain was a brave man, but the apparition, gleaming in the almost complete darkness, had been on him before he could do more than throw up his hands.

Jones had not finished. He went back to the chart-room and possibly even went on deck and took a look at the wheel. Then he went down again and killed the Hansen woman.

He was exceedingly cunning. He flung the ax into the room, and was up at the wheel again, all within a few seconds. To tear off and fold up the sheet, to hide it under near-by cordage, to strike the ship's bell and light his pipe — all this was a matter of two or three minutes. I had only time to look at Vail. When I got up to the wheel, Jones was smoking quietly.

I believe he tried to get Singleton

later, and failed. But he continued his devotions on the forward deck, visible when clad in his robe, invisible when he took it off. It was Jones, of course, who attacked Burns and secured the key to the captain's cabin; Jones who threw the ax overboard after hearing the crew tell that on its handle were finger-prints to identify the murderer; Jones who, while on guard in the after house below, had pushed the key to the storeroom under Turner's door; Jones who hung the marlinespike over the side, waiting perhaps for another chance at Singleton; Jones, in his devotional attire, who had frightened the crew into hysteria, and who, discovered by Mrs. Johns in the captain's cabin, had rushed by her, and out, with the ax, It is noticeable that he made no attempt to attack her. He killed only in obedience to his signal, and he had had no signal.

Perhaps the most curious thing, after the murderer was known, was the story of the people in the after house. It was months before I got that in full. The belief among the women was that Turner, maddened by drink and unreasoning jealousy, had killed Vail, and then, running amuck or discovered by the other victims, had killed them. This was borne out by Turner's condition. His hands and parts of his clothing were blood-stained.

Their condition was pitiable. Unable to speak for himself, he lay raving in his room, talking to Vail and complaining of a white figure that bothered him. The key that Elsa Lee picked up was another clue, and in their attempt to get rid of it I had foiled them. Mrs. Johns, an old friend and, as I have said, an ardent partisan, undertook to get rid of the ax, with the result that we know. Even Turner's recovery brought little courage. He could only recall that he had gone into Vail's room and tried to wake him, without result; that he did not know of the blood until the next day, or that Vail was dead; and that he had a vague recollection of something white and ghostly that night — he was not sure where he had seen it.

The failure of their attempt to get rid of the storeroom key was matched by their failure to smuggle Turner's linen off the ship. Singleton suspected Turner, and, with the skillful and not overscrupulous aid of his lawyer, had succeeded in finding in Mrs. Sloane's trunk the incriminating pieces.

As to the meaning of the keys, file, and club in Singleton's mattress, I believe the explanation is simple enough. He saw against him a strong case. He had little money and no influence, while Turner had both. I have every reason to believe that he hoped to make his escape before the ship anchored, and was frustrated by my discovery of the keys and by an extra bolt I put on his door and window.

The murders on the schooner-yacht *Ella* were solved.

McWhirter went back to his hospital, the day after our struggle, wearing a strip of plaster over the bridge of his nose and a new air of importance. The Turners went to New York soon after, and I was alone. I tried to put Elsa Lee out of my thoughts, as she had gone out of my life, and, receiving the hoped-for hospital appointment at that time, I tried to make up by hard work for a happiness that I had not lost because it had never been mine.

A curious thing has happened to me. I had thought this record finished, but perhaps —

Turner's health is bad. He and his wife and Miss Lee are going to Europe. He has asked me to go with him in my professional capacity!

It is more than a year since I have seen her.

The year has brought some changes. Singleton is again a member of the Turner forces, having signed a contract and a temperance pledge at the same sitting. Jones is in a hospital for the insane, where in the daytime he is a cheery old tar with twinkling eyes and a huge mustache, and where now and then, on Christmas and holidays, I send him a supply of tobacco. At night he sleeps in a room with opaque glass windows through which no heavenly signals can penetrate. He will not talk of his crimes — not that he so regards them — but now and then in the night he wraps the drapery of his couch about him and performs strange orisons in the little room that is his. And at such times an attendant watches outside his door.

Chapter 25

The Sea Again

Once more the swish of spray against the side of a ship, the tang of salt, the lift and fall of the rail against the sea-line on the horizon. And once more a girl, in white from neck to heel, facing into the wind as if she loved it, her crisp skirts flying, her hair blown back from her forehead in damp curls.

And I am not washing down the deck. With all the poise of white flannels and a good cigar, I am lounging in a deck-chair, watching her. Then —

"Come here!" I say.

"I am busy."

"You are not busy. You are disgracefully idle."

"Why do you want me?"

She comes closer, and looks down at me. She likes me to sit, so she may look

301

superior and scornful, this being impossible when one looks up. When she has approached —

"Just to show that I can order you about."

"I shall go back!" — with raised chin. How I remember that raised chin, and how (whisper it) I used to fear it!

"You cannot. I am holding the edge of your skirt."

"Ralph! And all the other passengers looking!"

"Then sit down — and, before you do, tuck that rug under my feet, will you?"

"Certainly not."

"Under my feet!"

She does it, under protest, whereon I release her skirts. She is sulky, quite distinctly sulky. I slide my hand under the rug into her lap. She ignores it.

"Now," I say calmly, "we are even. And you might as well hold my hand. Everyone thinks you are."

She brings her hands hastily from under her rug and puts them over her head. "I don't know what has got into you,'' she says coldly. ''And why are we even?''

''For that day you told me the deck was not clean.''

''It wasn't clean.''

''I think I am going to kiss you.''

''Ralph!''

''It is coming on. About the time that the bishop gets here, I shall lean over and —''

She eyes me, and sees determination in my face. She changes color.

''You wouldn't!''

''Wouldn't I!''

She rises hastily, and stands looking down at me. I am quite sure at that moment that she detests me, and I rather like it. There are always times when we detest the people we love.

''If you are going to be arbitrary just because you can —''

''Yes?''

''Marsh and the rest are in the smoking-room. Their sitting-room is empty.''

Quite calmly, as if we are going below for a clean handkerchief or a veil or a cigarette, we stroll down the great staircase of the liner to the Turners' sitting-room, and close the door.

And — I kiss her.